Romero
Pools

ALYSSA HALL

◆ FriesenPress

One Printers Way
Altona, MB R0G0B0,
Canada

www.friesenpress.com

ISBN
978-1-03-913117-0 (Hardcover)
978-1-03-913116-3 (Paperback)
978-1-03-913118-7 (eBook)

1. Fiction, Romance, Suspense

Distributed to the trade by The Ingram Book Company

Also by Alyssa Hall

Trusting Claire
Wanting Aidan

Love is a single soul inhabiting two bodies

Aristotle

Romero Pools features the return of
characters from both
Trusting Claire
and
Wanting Aidan

To learn more about these characters,
you can also read these books

1

It was a very warm day, as was typical for mid-November in southern Arizona. The sky was the shade of blue that could be seen splashed over travel magazines, enticing people to some desirable tropical destination. There was a paintbrush wisp of white cloud to the west. Marin had just finished her climb up the last gentle slope to the second pools and waterfall. She stepped across the rocks to the far side of the falls, where she collapsed on one of the big smooth rocks. She was tired. For some reason, the hike today seemed harder than usual. Lying on the hard cool surface, she closed her eyes and listened to the roar of the water as it cascaded over the boulders. Marin exhaled as she waited for her body to cool off. Before long, she had fallen asleep.

In her dream, she looked over to the passenger seat where Tyler sat smiling at her. The sun was shining on his face, and his hair was blowing across his forehead, partially obscuring his intense blue eyes. Suddenly, the scene exploded with the sound of busting metal and screeching tires. Marin woke up with a jolt. *Not again,* she thought. She had no idea how long she had been asleep, but she could tell by the shift of the sun that it had been too long. She would have to hurry to get back to the base of the mountain. She didn't like to leave it too late, as she would hate to be caught here even nearing dusk, let alone after dark. She picked up her small backpack, took a big drink of water, and stood to leave.

Marin quickly passed the lower falls, very aware of her aloneness. She was doubtlessly the last person on the trail. Again, she scolded herself for falling asleep. The days were considerably shorter in November, and she knew better than to leave it so late. Crossing the water using the stepping-stones, she easily made it over to the other side. Although the levels were higher this time of year, the rocks were not yet submerged. It wasn't unusual to cross over in ankle-deep water. Once safely on the other bank, she struck up the steep incline. The grogginess had dissipated and she was now fully awake. Her thoughts of Tyler and the crash began to subside.

Heading up the narrow path that twisted its way around boulders and small trees, Marin ascended up from the stream-bed and began the steep, rocky climb up the ridge. She would have to climb for about twenty minutes before the trail would level out somewhat before descending again, back towards the parking lots below. Hearing a disturbance from the top of the ridge above her, Marin looked up just as a few small rocks came down onto the path in front of her. She stopped in her tracks, worried about what might come down next. She wondered if it were an animal moving along the ledge above her. "Preferably a bighorn sheep and not a mountain lion," she mused aloud.

Suddenly, Marin heard a cracking of branches in the vegetation above. There was something big moving around up there. Her first thought was to pass by quickly and keep moving, but before she could react, a dark mass plummeted to the ground in front of her. She let out a low scream and froze in her tracks. She stood like that for a moment before she realized it wasn't an animal but a man. Marin stared at the figure, absorbing what had just happened. The body was not moving. Was he dead? She stood like that for a moment, waiting, although she didn't know what she was waiting for.

Snapping to her senses, Marin rushed forward. The man had fallen on his side and appeared to be unconscious, but she could tell he was still breathing. She noticed a large bloody patch on his forehead where it had struck a rock. Feeling flummoxed, Marin was unsure whether to try to move him, not knowing how badly he was hurt.

Marin cautiously looked around for a sign of anyone else. Was this man alone? She waited for a moment, listening. There was nothing but stillness. She then grabbed a small towel from her pack and knelt beside him. Moistening the towel with water from her bottle, she cooled his face and wiped the grime from his wound. Marin was afraid to breathe and was becoming worried when his eyelids suddenly fluttered. Slowly, his eyes started to blink open.

She looked at him with a worried smile and said, "Well, hello there."

The man looked confused for a moment, so Marin continued, "You just fell, from up there." She pointed upwards to the ridge.

"Oh shit. I did, didn't I?" His hand went up to his face, shielding his eyes. "I lost my footing. I took a wrong turn looking for the path down. I was trying to take a picture." He tried to move but winced in pain.

"What hurts?" she asked. "Aside from your head."

He laughed weakly. "Actually, I don't feel my head. But everything else hurts."

"I think you may have knocked yourself out. I need to put some pressure on your head, if I may. You are bleeding and I'd like to try to stop it," Marin said, as she wrapped her towel tightly around the wound and tucked it under his head to hold it in place. He lay still. "Should I check you for broken bones or anything?" she offered.

"Do you know how to do that?" he asked.

"Well, no, but I figured if I just pressed everything, you'd scream if I hit a sore spot. Isn't that how they do it on TV?"

The man was now starting to stir. "Well, no thanks. Let's just see if I can feel anything when I sit up. We'll start there, shall we?"

"Do you want some water?" Marin asked.

"Please. I have some in my pack, if you don't mind."

Marin fumbled with the bottle that was clipped to the side pocket of his backpack, which he was still wearing. With Marin's help, the man was now propped up on one elbow as he drank the now warm fluid. Turning his gaze upward, he looked at the ledge above.

"That was quite the fall. Thank Christ there was this path here, or I could have fallen a lot further. Thanks for your help, by the way." This time he looked straight at Marin and, with a smile, offered her an awkward handshake. "Hi, I'm Adam."

"And I'm Marin," she replied, sighing with some relief. She fumbled with the towel, which was sliding down into his eyes. The blood had subsided somewhat. "Can I help you stand? We might not be out of the woods just yet."

"Agreed," said Adam enthusiastically. "Let's get me up."

They locked elbows and Marin braced herself while she pulled back. After the second attempt, Adam struggled to his feet and very nearly collapsed again.

"Shit," he yelled. "My leg. And maybe my ribs, as well. No, definitely my ribs, too." He leaned on the rock face for support.

"Can you stand on your leg? Do you think it's broken or just sprained?" Marin didn't want to panic. There was a little more than two hours of light left, and they were most surely the last two on the trail at this time of day. She had seen nobody behind her. Not to mention the fact that they had no cell phone service and so could not call for help.

Adam put his hand on her shoulder for support and took a few steps forward, testing his legs. He winced in pain but did stay on his feet. "Okay, so I think it's safe to say it's not broken, which is the good news, right?"

Marin nodded in agreement. "So, I guess this means celebrations are in order. Woo-woo," she said, feebly, making a circular motion with her fist above her head. "Now, we just need to figure a way to get you back down."

"What do you mean, 'we'?" Adam looked at her with concern. "I can't expect you to hang around. You just head on your way, and when you get to the bottom, you can send someone up."

"Are you crazy? I can't leave you. You'd probably fall off another cliff. You're not very steady on your feet, and I see you don't have a hiking pole. We're going down together, no argument."

Adam smiled at her warmly. "This is really too kind. I will hold you back."

"We are going together, Adam, and that's that." Marin put her pack on and hesitantly pushed her small body against Adam's much bigger frame to lend support. She felt a little awkward standing so close to a stranger but knew he needed help. "Now, how will this work? Should I hold onto you, or will you lean on me?"

"I think it's best if I hang on to you. Can we try it this way to start?" Adam brushed the dust from his clothes, stood up straight and with a huge exhalation, took his first steps forward. "So far so good," he announced with a smile.

Marin knew the first part would be the worse, as they were still ascending and many sections were steep. She was also worried about the time but said nothing. Hopefully when the shock wore off, Adam would be able to walk a little quicker. She guided his steps carefully until she was sure he wouldn't stumble again. Both had fallen silent, the tension apparent. There was little doubt about the challenge ahead of them.

2

MORE THAN TWENTY MINUTES HAD PASSED, AND THEY HAD been walking in silence. Adam had struggled up the steep sections, but now walking across the even terrain along this stretch, his gait seemed smoother. Marin stopped to check the gash in his head, which miraculously had stopped bleeding and had already begun to congeal and harden. She inhaled quietly with relief.

"Hey, I have some ibuprofen in my pack, Marin. Do you think you can get it out for me?" Adam watched her as she walked around to his back. She was young, maybe early twenties? She had a cherubic face with plump cheeks, a small chin, and very big eyes. Her sandy blond hair was tied back in a braid, but wispy strands were falling out around her face. Today, she was his angel.

Marin brushed her hair from her eyes and raised herself up on her toes to reach the small bottle. She shook out two pills and handed them to Adam, who then leaned on a rock to swallow the pills with some water.

"How are we doing?" he asked.

"Not too bad. Do you know where we are?" She looked up into his face to try to read his expression.

"Not really, but I think we are close to descending, am I right?"

Marin smiled. He seemed fine. Alert, optimistic, and relatively upbeat, considering what he had been through. "Not quite there, but yes, we are close," she answered him.

Adam watched her curiously as they continued along the wider path. The vegetation along this section was lush, almost tropical. It reminded him of when he went climbing in Maui. Marin walked by his side, slightly ahead. He was leaning on her shoulder and was hoping he wasn't leaning too hard. He felt warmed by this young person's kindness and compassion, taken aback by her willingness to help him.

Wanting to feel more engaged, Adam spoke. "I guess I'm lucky that I almost fell on you." His laugh was soft and deep, and it came from his belly.

Marin said yes, it was lucky, because if she hadn't fallen asleep, she would have already passed by the spot where he fell. Although still concerned about the amount of light, she was beginning to feel slightly more optimistic that they would make it to the parking lot. If not before dusk, it would definitely be before dark.

"Did you hike up here alone?" Adam asked, for no particular reason.

"Yes, I did today. Usually, I come with my hiking group, about once or twice a month, so I know the trail well. But I also come every year on this day, specifically on the day after the El Tour de Tucson bike ride."

"I came here for that ride! This is my second year participating," Adam uttered in surprise. "Did you ride as well?"

Marin went quiet. "Actually, no I didn't. Not this year. My

fiancé and I rode, years ago. But I have not ridden in nearly three years."

They were quiet again as Adam slowed his step. His leg hurt, but he didn't want to alarm his companion. He was sure he tore something, or possibly fractured something. He berated himself for being so stupid, for wandering off the trail and falling. He could have killed himself. He looked ahead at the scenery. The view was beyond spectacular. On his way to the pools, he had not looked back, savouring the views on the upward climb. He purposely wanted to save this scenery for the trek back down, and he was not disappointed. All of Oro Valley stretched ahead of him. He could make out the residential communities, the sweeping washes and the small shopping centres.

He focused on his immediate surroundings. The imposing walls of the canyon were completely spattered with saguaro cacti, stretching thousands of feet above and below where they stood. There must be at least 4,000 of them. In the distance, he could see what he thought were the Tortolita Mountains. It was late afternoon, shadows were long, and lights were beginning to appear in the town below.

"Well, I might suggest that you don't come alone if today is any indication of what can go wrong," said Adam with some emphasis.

"Funny, we always think we are invincible, and me especially should know better," she agreed.

"Do you live here, Marin? I mean, it must be quite the place to live. It's so beautiful."

Marin nodded. "I live here, yes. I moved here about two years ago from Washington State. I was born and raised there, but I had the opportunity to visit this area a few times and I fell in love with the place." She added, "What about you, Adam? Do you live here?"

Adam smiled as he answered, "I'm a Canadian. I'm from just outside of Toronto. I have a step-cousin who lives in England, and on our trips to visit him, I fell in love with cycling. It's what drew me here, to these rides. I'm sorry, but I need to stop talking for a while, Marin."

Adam's breath came in gasps. The only other sound was the crunching gravel beneath their boots. The rocky crags were ideal for holding on to, allowing him to slightly ease his weight from Marin. It was less hot now that the sun had sunk in the sky. The air was clean, and the temperature was perfect.

After a few moments, Adam felt he needed to hear the sound of conversation. He needed to get off this mountain, and the distraction of Marin's voice was helping. "Tell me about your fiancé, Marin. Does he hike as well?"

"Tyler was wonderful but his parents never liked me. I was what you'd call a party girl. But I am a totally different person now, after the accident. It was over three years ago when it happened. I was nineteen, and Tyler had just turned twenty. We were celebrating the fact that he had just been signed to play for the Portland Timbers. It was their debut year in the MLS. He had been for a tryout that was very positive. Then later, they called him in the middle of the preseason games. They wanted him to go to a training camp session. It was late February, and I remember how cold it was. On the way home, we stopped to celebrate. I was maybe a little drunk, it was late, and we were tired. He'd had a few more than me and was a mess. I had gone through a spell when I drank more often than

not, but I had been doing better since meeting Tyler. Yet there
I was, driving. I was trying so hard to stay focused on the road,
but Tyler was being an idiot, poking me in the ribs. I looked
over at him to tell him to stop, and then I looked up and there
was this truck coming at me and I completely lost control of
the car. There may have been ice on the road." Marin slowed to
help Adam over a jutting rock. The gravel trail made a drastic
turn left and downward.

Once safely on their way, she continued, "Anyway, the
car left the road and crashed. I was told we were both in very
serious condition. I spent over a year recovering, and by then,
Tyler's family had moved away. I never saw him again. I have
no idea where they went."

Adam felt his heart miss a beat. "That's terrible! But didn't
you try to find where he went? He never contacted you again?"

"Well, apparently, Tyler died." Marin answered, almost
coldly. Adam detected cynicism in her voice. "My parents told
me much later, just as I was preparing to leave the hospital.
It's taken me all this time to come to terms with it. What was
strange, though, was how the family had gone. Moved away,
like they'd never existed. Tyler's dad was a contractor, and I
tried to Google his whereabouts but with no luck. His family
was quite wealthy, so they had no problem disappearing."
Marin slowed a bit, feeling Adam stumble. "But then, and I
don't usually talk about this, one day, months later, I swore
I overheard my dad talking to someone about Tyler. As if he
was alive. When I asked him, he said I was imagining it. It felt
like some kind of conspiracy, you know? My doctor says it's
just my brain acting up from the injury."

Adam felt himself fading. His head was throbbing, and it

was becoming harder to breathe. He needed to sit down. He could see the worry on Marin's face. Those big brown doe eyes stared at him intensely, and her bottom lip began to quiver.

"I'm sorry, Marin. Please just give me a minute."

"Adam, we just need to make it to the flat area, where the trail junction is. I will have a signal by then and I can call someone. If we're not out of here on time, they'll lock the gates." She took her phone from her pocket and instantly cried out in excitement. "Adam! I have a signal!" she said as she promptly dialed 911. With a frenetic excitement, Marin described the situation and their location. The dispatcher asked her to stay on the line so they could ping her phone to track their exact position. She carefully set her phone on a flat rock ledge beside her. Almost giddy, she helped Adam to his feet.

"Now, if we can just make it to the last descent towards Montrose Pools, they will be able to get to you easily. The dispatcher said it's a good area for the medics to drive into. Can you just go a little further, Adam? We have about half an hour to get there. It'll be getting dark by then, so we got really lucky."

Adam nodded his head and smiled weakly. They continued in silence, Marin growing more concerned for her companion, who had turned an ashy white. His forehead had started to bleed again. This section was so steep, Adam needed to sit on the rocks and lower himself on his bum. But then he started to hum a song.

"What is that?" she asked.

Smiling, he answered, "Just a little song I used to sing with my stepmother Claire. She has a funny little habit of singing herself through situations. She has a virtual disc jockey in her head. I grew up listening to her singing, and as the years went by and she was less familiar with the current music, I would start to make them up for her, or introduce new ones to her. It became a thing, and to a certain degree, I developed the same habit. I imagine if she were here, it's what she might have chosen."

"So, what are you singing now?" Marin asked, smiling.

"'I'm Still Standing.'" He chuckled. "But that's not mine, that's Elton and Bernie."

"You sound like a very intriguing person, Adam, and this has been a real nice experience getting to talk to you. Although under the circumstances, nice may not be the best word." The relief in her voice was noticeable.

In what seemed like mere minutes, they heard the sound of the emergency vehicle approaching from below. They had not covered the distance that Marin had hoped, but she sat Adam down on a rock and ran ahead to greet the rescue workers. The paramedics unloaded a two-wheeled trolley and scrambled up the rock to where Adam sat propped. After carefully immobilizing him on the stretcher, they slowly made their way back to the vehicle where Marin stood waiting.

As the three paramedics were loading Adam into the back, she asked, "Is there anyone I can call? Are you here alone? Oh—and what about your car?"

"No, there is no one. I'm here alone," answered Adam. His fatigue was apparent, and he looked depleted.

She turned to the paramedic, asking where they were taking him. As she suspected, the woman told Marin they would take Adam the short distance to Oro Valley Hospital.

"They are not taking you far. Give me your car keys, Adam.

I'll call my girlfriend Penelope. She will come and we'll bring your car to the hospital. I'll bring your keys back up to you."

Adam, in his current state, didn't have the luxury of time in considering how safe it was to hand his car keys over to a perfect stranger. "They're in my backpack, Marin. Front pocket. You really think of everything, don't you? I suppose that's lucky for me. I'll never be able to thank you," said Adam.

She squeezed his arm and smiled. "Shut up, Adam."

Then the ambulance doors closed.

3

ADAM HAD NEVER THOUGHT HE COULD BE THIS HAPPY IN A hospital bed, but he melted into the sheets, imagining these were the finest linens in the best five-star hotel in town. The white waffle hospital blanket seemed like the finest goose-down duvet. Since being brought in, he had been gently poked, prodded, X-rayed, cleaned up, and drugged. Now, he was ready to sleep, and that he did.

He had been woken a few times during the night, as was protocol for one concussed, but when it was deemed safe to do so, he had been permitted to sleep for longer. He had slept deeply and was now waking up to the sound of a nurse moving beside his bed. The lights were dimmed, and the hallways were quiet. She was changing his IV drip and, seeing his eyes open, informed him that an entire day had passed.

"You have been sleeping the sleep of the dead, Mr. Wyner. The nurses have come in frequently to check on you, but you were so peaceful and all of your vital signs were good, so after the third wake-up, we weren't concerned. How do you feel?" asked the tall, freckled brunette.

"Actually, I'm starving," was his response. "I feel like I could eat a horse."

"Well, would you settle for some toast and maybe some pudding?"

"Are you serious?" Adam twisted his face into a grimace. As he spoke, he realized the grogginess had not fully left him; his words had come out in a slur.

"It's all I can get you now, until the evening meal," was the nurse's tepid response. Finishing with the IV, she grabbed the empty bag with short, terse movements. Placing everything on her small tray, she pushed it backwards and prepared to leave the room.

Adam had been kidding and was now regretting his hasty response. This woman had no sense of humour. Mustering up a smile, he answered with, "I'm sorry. I'd love some toast, please!" He figured he better speak up quickly before she left and brought him nothing.

Just then, there was a knock on the door and in peered a familiar face. It was Marin. Only she looked very different than she had on the mountain. She was smartly dressed in check-ered pants and a pale-yellow blouse. Her hair, while tied back in a freshly plaited braid, still had wispy loose strands around her face. Gone was the worried expression.

"Hey there," she whispered as she slowly stepped towards the bed. "May I come in?"

"Please do." Adam tried to sit up slightly but winced in pain, so remained where he was. He was still feeling woozy, either from too much sleep or the meds.

The nurse directed Marin to the chair beside the bed. "You might have to leave if the doctor comes. He's making his rounds, and he's not had a chance to speak to the patient yet." Looking at Adam, she smiled and said, "I'll be right back with your toast."

Smiling at the nurse, Marin sat down and regarded Adam with a worried expression on her face. "How do you feel? I thought a lot about you last night. You had an awful fall yesterday. I can still see the image of you, the way you landed. Makes me shudder."

"Well, my head feels like it's grown a few sizes, but otherwise, I feel not too bad. I know I will feel worse later, as I'm sure I'm fairly drugged up right now."

"That's almost a guarantee," she agreed. "By the way, where are you staying? I mean, where will you go when you are released?" Marin asked.

"I'm staying at the Hotel Congress, right downtown. Did you know it was haunted? A friend told me about it last year, so I thought I'd give it a try. So far, no ghosts, although it doesn't help that I've not been there for the past two nights." Winking at her, Adam added, "I also chose that hotel because I wanted to be near the start line of the ride, at Armory Park."

"Wow, isn't that the place where John Dillinger hung out? It's ancient, that building. But, why did you come all the way out here to Catalina State Park? You could have gone hiking in Sabino Canyon, or Pima Canyon."

"I heard it was a wonderful hike, up to the pools. And it was, for the most part," Adam said with an almost sardonic sounding chuckle.

Marin fumbled in her purse as he spoke. "Before I forget, here's your car key. We brought your car here to the hospital last night. It's parked at the end of the first row, to your right. I thought it might be helpful to know. It's a pretty big parking lot."

Adam looked at the key in her hand. He hadn't thought about what he would do. He needed to see the doctor so he could get an idea of what the hell was wrong with him. He needed to leave. He had a plane to catch tomorrow. Or was it today? This wasn't good.

"Well, I'll just set it here on your night stand."

"I'm sorry. Thank you, of course. I'm just trying to plan my next move, which is pretty funny considering it hurts to move." He relaxed when she smiled.

"I hadn't heard it was haunted," Marin said. "Did you just make that up?"

"No, but I think someone made it up. I'm sure for publicity, but many believe it to be true. I must admit, walking down that long dark corridor I did feel a bit like Jack Nicholson in *The Shining*," Adam joked, but then added more seriously, "It's a very old hotel, early 1900s. It's noisy, and there's no TV in the room, but it's beautiful inside. I find it very fascinating, and it has an appeal. It's more like a museum, really."

In what seemed like no time, the nurse reappeared with a small tray. "Here you go, toast and pudding. May you dine like a king. The doctor should be here within a few minutes. I'm sorry, but your friend might have to move to the waiting room."

Adam looked at the small, cold slice of white toast with the pat of hard butter before him on the yellowing plastic tray and let out an audible sound, something between a sigh and a moan. "When I get out of here, Marin, I want to go out for a nice meal. And I want you to join me, to thank you for all your help."

Before Marin had the chance to respond, the doctor came into the room. She promptly stood up and left, nodding at the doctor as she passed him.

* * * *

WALKING TO THE WAITING AREA, Marin checked her watch. She would need to go back to work shortly. She knew it wasn't her concern, but she was curious to hear what the doctor said. Just how injured was Adam? He needed to worry about his car, his hotel room, his return flight to Toronto . . . all these things. What if he wasn't well enough to travel?

She sat down near the window and absentmindedly grabbed a magazine from the table. It sat on her lap, unopened, as she stared out the window at the Catalina Mountains. She thought about Adam falling, her shock at seeing him lying on the ground. She closed her eyes and daydreamed.

Marin's eyes few open, and she lifted her head. She looked up at the clock on the wall to check the time. Fifteen minutes had passed, and she needed to leave. Walking back down the hallway, she saw that Adam's door was still shut. Stopping at the nurses' station, she leaned over the counter and asked the nurse to please let Adam know she had to leave but would be back in the evening. Then she turned and hurried down the staircase. Exiting the building, Marin squinted against the bright Arizona sun. It was another hot day.

It would take her about fifteen minutes to get back to her office, and she didn't want to be late. Marin loved her job at the *Tucson Weekly* newspaper. After completing courses in journalism, she spent some time writing for a community circular and an online blog. She quickly became known, as her writing skills were excellent, and she had an exceptional rapport with people. As a result, Marin was fortunate enough to land this new position as a reporter. She had applied online and was hired over a video chat. She had packed her bags and moved right away, having been doubly fortunate in finding a place to stay almost right away.

Her current position was temporary and she was still in a trial phase, but she loved it and was prepared to do what was needed to further her career. There was a fair bit of grunt work to contend with, but Marin did manage to go on assignments on occasion, to fact check or conduct simple interviews. She was getting better at these, as she was slowly getting accustomed to her new way of life here in southern Arizona.

Marin was in the process of working her way up to a junior editor, a position that would be available in less than a year. Peter was retiring, and when it had been announced, Marin's superior had taken her aside, suggesting she work hard and prepare herself to apply for the posting. Based more on her reputation rather than qualifications, she was doing a good job thus far, proving her competence.

As Marin drove out onto the main road, her gaze instinctively turned to the Catalinas. And as usual, her thoughts returned to Tyler and the omnipresent feeling of wishing he was here. Turning right, she headed along North Oracle Road and towards her office.

4

IT WAS A LITTLE PAST SEVEN BUT ALREADY DARK WHEN Marin walked into Adam's room. He looked at her with a mixture of relief and gratitude. "Again, you've saved me. Thanks for coming back; I thought I'd die of boredom." He shifted his position amidst the stack of pillows.

"I tried to come back earlier, but you were still with the doctor. So, what did he say? Only good news, I hope." Marin resumed her place in the same chair by his bed.

"Well, I had a concussion, which didn't surprise the doctor given the size of my head wound. He said it could have been much worse. I have a few cracked ribs, which is why it hurts to move. I also have a Grade Two thigh contusion. But the good news is that he will discharge me tomorrow so I can go home. I had to promise that I wouldn't attempt a marathon in the next few weeks."

"Oh, Adam, I am so relieved. That's really good news."

"Yes, so I called the hotel and booked an extra night, and I was able to change my flight. So, I was thinking about it, and I want to ask if you are free to join me for a meal tomorrow evening, at the Congress?" he asked. "I'd love to thank you for what you've done for me."

"Oh, gee, I don't know. I'll have to check my calendar," Marin answered with obvious sarcasm. "But really, you don't have to thank me."

"Okay then, just come as my friend, seeing me off. I'm on a nine-forty flight tomorrow evening, so it will be an early meal, as I have to head out right afterwards. I have a late checkout, at four, so maybe come to the hotel around five? They have great eating options there. I can meet you at the bar?"

"Thanks, Adam, that sounds nice." Marin cleared her throat before continuing. "Hope you don't mind, but I was thinking about something you were talking about just before the rescue workers came. You were talking about your stepmom and her songs. Are you two close? What I mean is, how old were you when your mom and dad split? Were you close to your real mom? I hated mine."

"My mom left before I was even two, so I didn't know her at all," said Adam. "For many years, it was just myself and my dad. But then, when I was about six, my dad met this amazing woman. I remember we went to England to visit her family, and after that, things changed. She became a big part of our lives. Before that, I never knew what it was like to have a mom. My dad had become my universe—the whole shebang. He raised me alone and never made it look like work. But my stepmom Claire has been the best mom I could have asked for."

"Well, mine may as well have left me. I was invisible to her, and she was callous and uncaring. She lived in her own little world. Now I understand why some men might be tempted to go it alone. I think my parents hated each other."

"Whoa, Marin, you should never say things like that. How bad could it be?"

"Well, amongst other things, my mom was a closet drinker. She never worked, and as long as I can remember, she always had a glass in her hand. Well, that's not entirely true. She seemed to not drink when we still lived in Tacoma. But when we moved to Kirkland, she went funny. And before long, I'd notice that she would disappear to the spare bedroom for long periods of time. Once I went in there and started digging around and I found her bottle stash. So, I used to take some of it from time to time, when I was going out with my friends. Am I talking too much?"

"No, I asked you to talk. Please go on."

"Okay, well, she caught me eventually and gave me her version of a scolding. But I stood up to her and said, 'What are you going to do, tell Dad?' She realized she couldn't say anything because I'd have told Dad about her. So, we really avoided each other after that. Dad was too busy to notice anything, and I was older by then and rarely home anyway. But I did notice things were a bit off between Mom and Dad. They never did pay much attention to me, but now, it seemed more obvious. It was, like, almost deliberate. I was at a point where I basically looked after myself, so I didn't give a shit about what they were going through."

She sat back, a smile breaking over her face. "By then I met Tyler. I mean, I already knew him; we hung out with the same group of friends. But by then, we really noticed each other. We would break away from the gang to spend time together. Next thing I knew, we couldn't bear to be apart." She shifted in her chair and looked embarrassed. "This is awful. I'm not here to talk about me. How did you make me do that?"

Adam laughed. "I'm sorry. Occupational hazard. I'm a

youth counsellor. Actually, I'm a psychologist. I get carried away with questioning. But please, I really want to hear about you and Tyler."

She smiled and looked up to the ceiling. "He was my universe as well. The whole shebang, as you said. He was a very good soccer player. I remember the reason we first came to Tucson. He was trying out with a Portland team, and we flew here to Tucson for the weekend. Did I tell you already? It was during that trip we climbed to Romero Pools and he asked me to marry him. We went back home, and out of the blue, we began to conduct ourselves differently. Sure, we still partied with our friends, but we were both somehow more subdued. Our priorities shifted without really having talked about it. We seemed to grow up over night and were more serious."

Marin stood up to help Adam with his pillow, which had slipped out from under his shoulder, then sat down to continue. "Tyler's parents were naturally furious about the engagement and did everything they could to talk Tyler out of it. That's when my parents started acting weird as well. I couldn't understand it. Tyler was a really good guy. Anyone would be proud to call him a friend. He was smart, motivated, and sincere."

"I'm curious why you would say that they were naturally upset? Why is that?"

"Oh, his dad, Keith, hated me! Right from day one. His mom says it was because I was a wild child, but it seemed like something worse than that, the way he acted. Tyler said he always tried to control him, and that was just one more way to do it. But I saw something different in his eyes whenever he looked at me. I was not allowed to go to his house. Tyler always came to mine, and we tried hard to avoid his dad when we were out and around the town. The truth is, I was really afraid of his dad. And I think Tyler was as well. His dad had a bad reputation from what I heard, and he had a very bad temper. I wouldn't put anything past him."

"Well, I know parents can get very protective. You said you were just nineteen? Maybe he thought you were too young to be engaged?" was all Adam could think of to say.

"Well, Tyler said his mom was married the day she turned twenty, and that he was born only a few months after that. And I know my parents married quite young as well. Lots of people do! My best friend's parents were only nineteen when they had her. But we weren't getting married or anything. I mean, shit, engaged is not married, is it?"

Adam nodded his head in agreement as he pushed the dial on his bed to recline it slightly, in an effort to relieve some of his discomfort. The pain in his leg was returning.

"Then we had the trip to Portland." Marin fell silent and looked out the window. "It's getting late, I should go. You look tired."

"Please, Marin, just stay a while longer. I'd like to try to stay awake for as long as I can. Could you finish the story?"

"I want you to understand that I don't really drink any more than anyone else. It was just the time. Mostly, it was rebellion against my mom. But that night, we had drunk a lot. It was so long ago, but I remember it like yesterday. We were almost home and had stopped at a bar to rest and to eat something. I guess Tyler drank a bit more than he ate. But he was excited and this was a real celebration. So, we decided I would drive us home, being the more sober one. I don't know what to say about the accident, but we were smashed up pretty bad. When I regained consciousness, which I hear was many months later, I was focusing on recovering. My questions about Tyler's condition went mostly unanswered."

"Was anyone else hurt in the accident, Marin?"

She shook her head. "No, the police officer who came to see me in the hospital after I woke up said we rolled over into a ditch, then hit a wall of rock. We were just half an hour from home. When I did finally wake up, I cried, I was so afraid. I was completely bandaged up and couldn't move. Everyone had waited a long time to be able to ask me about the accident, but a lot of good that did, as I hardly remembered anything. It wasn't until I was moved to a regular ward, I don't know how many months later, that they told me Tyler was dead."

Marin sat in her chair, perched on the edge, causing the back legs to slightly lift off the ground. She absent-mindedly played with the strap on her purse as she let out a sigh. It was a sigh that told a story of heartache, regret, and loss. "Anyway, I need to stop talking about it." Looking straight at Adam, she blurted out, "I think if anyone wanted to do anything for me, they'd help me find out where he is. Somewhere out there is either a being or a grave. I tried my best researching; I searched every state website, looking for death records. Why is there nothing there? If he's dead, there would be a record somewhere, wouldn't there? But if he's alive, where is he? I haven't heard from him. All I ask is to know what happened to him."

Marin looked sheepish as she became aware of the fierceness with which she spoke, and her voice softened. "It's Tyler's birthday in April. It's beautiful up in the mountains in April,

Adam. There's nothing like the desert in the spring when everything is in bloom. The desert comes alive with so much colour, and the air is so fresh."

Adam marveled at the way Marin's entire persona transformed as she began speaking of the desert and the spring bloom. "I'd like to see it in the spring," he said, feeling it was the right thing to say.

"Well, maybe you could come back and hike to Romero Pools with me. You could join me on my last trip up. I will hike to the pools on that day and then I'll never go back. You see, Adam, I'm not unhappy. It has nothing to do with that anymore. I can walk around happy and involved, engaged. I have friends, a job, I'm in therapy—but to some extent, I am just a hollow shell. I have no drive, no soul, no real vision of a future."

"You might not always feel like that, Marin. We do heal," offered Adam.

"Yes, you are right. We do. That's my point. I need to heal and I need to move on. I now approach everything with a realism and appreciation that I never had before. It took years of therapy—physical and mental—for me to get my head on right. Some closure would be good. My old dreams have faded, but I need to find new ones."

Glancing at the clock on the wall as she spoke, she jumped to her feet. "I have to go, Adam. There's some place I need to be. I can come back in the morning if you like, to see if you need anything?"

Adam shook his head. "I'll see you for dinner tomorrow, Marin. You've done enough for me already. I think I can get out of here by myself. And I will think about it, about coming back in April."

With that, Marin grabbed her bag and headed for the door, turning to smile at him as she disappeared into the corridor. "See you tomorrow," she said, into the air. Although Adam was tired, he had a few texts to send. The first was to his dad, Ben, who would no doubt be waiting for an update, the other was to Sofia.

5

ADAM WAS DISCHARGED JUST BEFORE NOON, HAVING received his final instructions from the doctor. One of the nurses came into the room with his bag of belongings. He felt weak and unsteady on his feet as he stood up to go to and have a wash. Coming back to his bed, Adam noticed that the nurse had closed his curtain to give him some privacy while he dressed. He opened the plastic bag of belongings and let out a low groan as he examined the contents. Realizing he had nothing else to wear, he reluctantly put his grubby hiking clothes back on. They were dusty and smelled of sweat. There was blood on the shoulder of his shirt, and his pants were torn. He never thought to get a change of clothes, but then again, the opportunity to go shopping hadn't exactly presented itself.

Struggling into his clothes, Adam almost regretted his refusal of assistance in getting dressed. At last, he opened the curtain and sat in the chair, waiting for further instructions. Adam found all the nurses to be extremely attentive and courteous as they warmly bid him goodbye. Just as Adam prepared to walk away, a smiling orderly appeared with a wheelchair, causing Adam to groan.

"You want me to sit in that chair, don't you?" he lamented.

The orderly laughed. "Why do I always get that response when I show up with the chair? Sorry, bud, them's the rules."

Adam sat with his bag of belongings in his lap while the orderly wheeled him to the parking lot to where his car sat baking in the noonday sun. The hot Arizona air hit Adam like a blowtorch. He sensed he would miss this heat once he was back in Toronto. Now relaxed, Adam lowered himself gingerly into his car, extremely relieved to be out of the hospital, as nice as the staff had been.

"Are you sure you can drive?" asked the concerned orderly.

"We'll see soon enough," Adam answered with feigned nonchalance. He was leaving no matter what.

The orderly shook his hand and walked back towards the building, whistling.

Finding his sunglasses, Adam started the engine and put the car in gear. Driving wasn't as bad as he feared it might be, as there was very little traffic on the road, so braking was minimal. The rental company had agreed to retrieve the car from the hotel, and Adam had allowed himself ample time to get there before someone arrived to pick it up. Driving along Oracle, he looked up to the 5,000-foot-high rock cliffs of Pusch Ridge on his left, not wanting to think about what might have happened to him had Marin not been up in the mountains that day. He turned his eyes to the road ahead, feeling grateful. It was time to say goodbye to Oro Valley.

Once back at the hotel, the valet greeted Adam at the door before taking the car away. Rather than heading straight to his room, he wandered outside towards Maynard's Patio, where he had decided to have a sandwich and a beer. Just as the hostess approached him, he suddenly remembered his shirt was covered in old blood. Holding up his index finger to motion that he'd be right back, Adam walked back out to the street.

Looking around, he spotted only one small gift shop. He reluctantly entered, in search of clothing, but all he found was a souvenir tee shirt. Pocketing his receipt, he quickly changed and, leaving the shop, disposed of the stained shirt in nearby waste receptacle situated in front of the hotel. Without dwelling on whether the shirt fit properly, Adam returned to Maynard's and was directed to a table. The hostess smiled at his new shirt. He hadn't noticed what it said, and quite frankly didn't have the energy to care.

Adam loved the vibrancy of this place. For him, it wouldn't be easy leaving this city. Once satiated and feeling suddenly very stiff, Adam stood to leave, noticing more blood on his pant leg. Groaning under his breath, he clumsily made his way to his room to begin the slow process of packing his belongings. He was disappointed that he wouldn't be able to have one last stroll along the historic Fourth Avenue, with its funky shops and colourful characters. But every part of him hurt. Grateful that he had time for a quick nap, Adam fell asleep very quickly.

The shrill sound of the Amtrak train whistle right outside his window jolted Adam awake. He eased himself from the bed to check the time before heading to the bathroom. Adam was still smiling to himself about his tee shirt, which he had studied more closely upon returning to his room. It read, *Arizona Girl*. He decided he would give it to Sofia.

After showering, he managed to tenderly clothe himself with clean travelling attire and called for the porter to help with his luggage. Adam found it perversely humorous that he couldn't handle the gear on his own. One remaining problem was to speak with the manager to figure out a way to store his luggage until the airport shuttle came.

By now, Adam was overcome with the anticipated melancholy as he realized his stay was over. He couldn't explain the scope of the mood, but he put it down to his physical state, not to mention the drugs. Reluctantly, with everything in order, this Arizona girl was finally ready to check out and settle his bill.

Now in the hotel bar, he glanced at his watch. It was past five thirty. Did Marin think he said six? He was certain he said five. He was unsure whether to order another beer, but decided to wait until Marin arrived. With a groan, Adam realized he couldn't call her even if he wanted to. It had been a careless oversight, not asking for her contact information. He didn't know her last name and he had no number for her. A huge mistake on his part, but he also realized that Marin hadn't offered her information or asked for his either. Growing increasingly perplexed by her absence, he speculated on another angle—perhaps she felt uncomfortable coming here to eat with him. He hadn't thought of that. He was, after all, a stranger.

By quarter past six, he headed to the outdoor restaurant and had a quick bite to eat. Adam again checked his watch. The airport shuttle would be here in less than an hour. When the waiter brought the bill, Adam asked if he could leave a note with him, in case someone came looking. He explained to the waiter that she might simply be late, but unfortunately, he had to leave. The waiter agreed and left a blank slip of paper on the small plastic tray along with the bill. Paying the bill, Adam sat until it was time to leave, sipping his water and enjoying the music and the activity around him. He wrote a short note to Marin and wedged it beneath the tray. As he stood to leave, he softly whispered a mental goodbye to the desert, to this magical place.

There was something about Tucson that he couldn't put into words. He could easily see why Marin moved here. There was a soul healing vibe about the place. As he left the patio, he didn't notice the gust of wind behind him. Nor did he notice the small slip of paper that had been wedged beneath the tray now being carried away on the breeze. Down the hill it went, fluttering in the wind and towards the train tracks.

Adam waited for the airline agent to unload his bicycle and suitcases onto the conveyor belt, and before long, he was heading towards the gate. To be walking with a cane felt foreign to him, and it seemed to take forever. He was in discomfort and it must have shown, for as soon as he reached the lounge, the steward came over and asked him if he'd like to pre-board the plane. Gratefully, Adam agreed. He needed to sit down. What was unexpected was the wheelchair, but he lowered himself willingly into the chair and waited to be rolled on to the plane.

A deep furrow had fixed itself between Adam's brows as he settled into his seat. But his mind was not on himself; he was curious about what had happened to Marin. Hopefully, it was simply her reluctance to meet a stranger and nothing more serious. He would have enjoyed continuing the conversation with her. He found her story compelling and Marin a very interesting and engaging young woman.

He made a mental note to always get contact information whenever he had plans with someone. What did she say her last name was? Or did she? Humming a tune, he closed his eyes. Before long he was fast asleep, unaware that the plane was leaving the ground.

6

Marin's day started out normal enough. She had been excited about the dinner engagement with Adam at five that evening and was looking forward to more conversation. Then just after two, her phone had rung. Marin was a little surprised to hear her editor's voice, calling to send her on assignment. Her editor needed Marin to drive to Green Valley of all places, to run a fact-check and produce a follow up story that would be featured in tomorrow's paper. A call that would normally have pleased her, but today she felt dread. This assignment could take hours.

"There's nobody else than can do it, Marin. Everyone is on assignment. It's been busy, particularly after El Tour and dealing with the aftermath. I appreciate this is your first year handling this event and you have no idea what it's like, but we have stories on the winners, the injured, the spectators, sponsors, and the traffic jams. Plus, the every day news stories as well, this being one of them." Sensing Marin's hesitation, the editor added, "This assignment will be good for you, Marin. So take it. See you when you get back."

A reluctant Marin went out to the parking lot and walked to the far end of the lot. She had a favourite spot where she liked to park her car, in the shade of a giant sycamore tree. Shade was a scarcity in most places, as large trees were limited in many parts of the city. Climbing in, she rolled the windows down and blasted the air conditioning. Still somewhat taken aback, she pulled out onto the road and headed in the direction of Green Valley, her excitement mixed with discouragement. She felt unprepared, not certain of where she was going, and knowing very little about the story. Above all else she wanted to be back in time for her visit with Adam.

Green Valley was twenty miles south of Tucson and was not so much a town as it was a community. Marin learned that places like this were designated CDP, or unincorporated. The latest population count in Green Valley had been twenty thousand but was slowly rising due to the growing popularity of the area, mostly with retirees and snowbirds. Marin made good time and arrived a few minutes before she was due at her destination. Driving through the streets, Marin looked around at the many home and town home complexes, some of them seeming to have appeared since she was last here. There were only two schools in Green Valley, as children at this point in time made up only two percent of the population.

The reason for her visit today was to cover a story about two bears that had been terrorizing hikers. The story had the potential of being interesting to readers if Marin could create the right tone. She really was grateful for the opportunity to be here. She needed to work on her interviewing skills, and this was the perfect chance. Now that she'd had a good look around the area, she was ready to get to it. Aware that she needed to get back in time to make tomorrow's paper, she hurried over to the address. But there also came the realization she may not make it back in time to see Adam, and she needed a moment to try to deal with that. Parking within the complex, Marin took out her cell phone and looked up the number for the Congress hotel. As the phone was ringing, she realized she had another problem: she had no idea what Adam's last name was.

When the desk clerk answered, she gave it a shot. "Hi, I'm trying to reach a guest of yours, whom I'm supposed to meet in an hour. His name is Adam, and I'm sorry but I don't know his last name. Can you please let me know if he's still in his room? I need to get a message to him, to say I'll be late."

"I'm sorry, but I don't think I can give out the names of guests. Besides, it's late and all guests would have checked out by now."

"Okay," answered Marin. "That's fair enough, thank you. But in case you do recall a guest named Adam, and you see him before he leaves the building, can you please pass my number on to him?"

The clerk was very kind and he took down Marin's number, although he would not confirm whether or not Adam was still there. Asking to be transferred to the bar, Marin was put on hold before her call was answered. She nervously tapped on her steering wheel, as the longer she was on the phone, the later she would be finished here. The girl who answered was far from cheerful, and the background music was loud. She didn't see anyone alone who looked as though they were waiting for someone.

"He is quite tall, and he's about thirtyish, I'd say, and he has dark hair combed back."

"I don't see anyone who looks like that," the girl snapped. "Look, I'm kinda busy here."

"Can you please look again?" Marin went on to describe Adam as a cross between Patrick Dempsey and Oliver Hudson.

"I don't know who they are either. Do they eat here often?" was the snide response.

"Never mind," Marin said, feeling very frustrated. She ended the call and closed her eyes for a moment. She tried not to think about it as she grabbed her gear and frowned. No shady tree to park under. Climbing out of her car, she walked to the building. It was a calm afternoon, with not a hint of breeze. The air smelled dry. As she approached the homes, she caught a breath of moisture from the sprinklers that were watering the lush foliage in the gardens ahead. Marin was uncharacteristically nervous. She dropped her journal and hoped that nobody was watching through the window. "You can do this," she said to herself, trying to focus.

The interviews went well. Spotting bears was not exactly an everyday occurrence in populated areas of southern Arizona. While these hikers were afraid of the bears, it turned out they didn't get very close. It was true the bears had followed them down the trails into the residential area, but they hadn't exactly been on their heels. The hikers had relaxed once safely indoors, and right away had called the media. The bears had stayed for quite a while, swimming in the pools, rooting around the yards, etc. That, to Marin, was the real story.

Although the hikers had not been in any immediate danger, their fear lay in the unpredictability of these dangerous animals. Many of the residents often eat outdoors, and some had not cleaned the barbecues. So, with the smell of food present from the grills and from around the outdoor furniture, there was the potential for trouble. Rangers were eventually called, but fortunately, the bears left of their own accord. If bears lose their fear of humans, they can become extremely dangerous and would need to be removed.

One hiker, Debbie, was unnecessarily distraught, seeing as how, she admitted, she didn't actually see a bear. Marin felt she was overplaying the anxiety card, seeming only to want her name in the paper. But Marin was sure to be appropriately and actively engaged as Debbie told her story. The hikers shared their photos with Marin, hoping to have them included in the story. Her interviews were now completed. Standing, Marin smiled as she put away her notepad while thanking everyone as she prepared to leave.

Knowing it was late, she hurried and stupidly spun her tires leaving the complex. Again, she hoped no one had been watching. Marin could only hope that Adam had waited, not remembering when he needed to be at the airport. Traffic was not great, and the freeway became bogged down as she neared the merge on to Highway 10. She crawled along until she got to the Congress Street exit, where she began to lose hope of catching Adam. Finding parking, she locked her car and literally ran all the way to the hotel.

Walking directly out to the patio, she realized right away she wouldn't see him. It was cold and dark, with not soul in sight. She went indoors to the bar and looked there as well. Determined, she took one last look around the area, all hope fading. She now needed to admit that Adam was gone and she might never see him again. She would have enjoyed getting to know him better, as he was indeed an interesting man. Speaking to no one, she turned and left the building.

Walking back to her car, Marin felt herself on the verge of

tears, although she wasn't sure why she was so emotional. For some incomprehensible reason, she felt as if she had missed out on something significant. This was confounding her usually sound judgment. She didn't even know the man, yet she felt some sort of loss. Adam had been so easy to talk to, and he seemed to understand her without the need to judge her. There was something about him, the kindness in his voice and the warmth in his eyes. It would have been nice to have dinner and spend a few more hours with him. She felt like she could have told him everything. Marin hadn't felt this level of grief since, well, since then.

7

ADAM WAS AGAIN UNCOMFORTABLE WITH THE WHEELCHAIR ride to the arrivals lounge, yet he was grateful for the lift, knowing it would be the last time he needed the help. He found it amazing and somewhat disheartening at how people gawked at him with more curiosity than caring. He kept his eyes down not wanting to meet their stares. Adam had taken some pain meds on the plane and still felt groggy as he was trying to fully wake up. He spotted his father in the crowd, a rather concerned look on his face. He waved at his dad, trying hard to look cheerful and nonchalant. Wheelchair? What wheelchair? As quickly as he could, he stood up and thanked the porter.

Ben hugged his son warmly, being careful not to squeeze too tightly. With scarcely a word, they headed to the baggage claim area, Ben's arm firmly locked through his son's.

"You look tired," said Ben at last, as he took stock of Adam. They were standing by the baggage carousel, which had not yet started moving.

Adam smiled. "Well, I slept for the majority of the flight. It's partly confusion, pain, and some regret for having been so careless. Let's throw in a bit of jet lag as well. I'll tell you all about it on the drive home." He was looking forward to being at his own home and taking a few days to absorb what he had been through. His thoughts were muddled, and he hardly felt like having this conversation. At that moment, a loud buzzer sounded and the carousel slowly creaked into motion.

Once Adam was settled into the vehicle, his gear safely stored in the trunk, Ben pulled out of the underground parkade and into the daylight. Adam made note of the surroundings. Pearson Airport in late November. Crap. It was snowing, which didn't surprise him. Banks of previously piled snow along the roadsides showed Adam the extent of what had been falling over the past few days. This was such a far cry from the warmth and dryness of Arizona. Adam again became aware of how much he would miss the desert air, the warm breezes. He shivered involuntarily at the sight of the frozen landscape.

Adam looked over at his father, a frown on his face. "We live in the wrong place. Don't you ever long for something warmer in the winter?"

"We've thought about Vancouver, to be closer to Claire's mom, but so far, it's just an idea that never happened," answered Ben, smiling at his son's scowl. Ben's wife was Claire Perova, a longstanding love whom he married when Adam was eight years old. Adam's mother had abandoned him and his father when Adam was a baby. Her whereabouts had never been discovered, and she had made no efforts to reconnect with Ben or Adam, who was now in his early thirties. Although it got easier over the years, both men thought of her from time to time, referring to different situations as being either before Mom or after Mom.

From a very early age, Adam had taken on the role of

nurturer to his father, whom he loved so much. It hadn't been easy watching his dad struggle at times, doing everything alone. Ben had not been able to convince Adam that raising him alone was never a struggle but an absolute blessing. He called it a gratifying pleasure, and it had filled his life with joy.

Claire and his dad had dated for a few years previous to getting married. Adam couldn't have been happier; he had been urging them for a very long time. Claire was the model stepmom, as she considered her role as being there for Ben and not to take over with Adam's raising. As a result of this, he had warmed to her and they had bonded quickly, although he always called her Claire and not Mom. She had no children, and she and Ben agreed to not have any of their own.

Theirs was a happy household. Claire filled their lives with music, laughter, and good food. She was always ready with her camera, which was never far from her reach, given her job as a real estate photographer. Adam remembered his dad in earlier days as quite reserved and thoughtful, but Claire, over the years, had brought out a previously unseen side of him.

"Vancouver wouldn't be such a bad idea, Dad. I'd come often, to check out the wineries and breweries. Winter out west sounds a hell of a lot better than winters here."

"I'm not disagreeing with you. It's just that right now we feel settled. Speaking of settled, am I taking you to your place, or bringing you home with me for a few days?" asked Ben. "I know Claire would love to see you. She's cooked up a storm. She left a pot of food at your place and made a pot at ours, not knowing where you'd want to be."

Adam laughed aloud, his first real laugh since his mishap. "That was very thoughtful of her, Dad, but I think I'll choose the pot at my place. I just need some time."

"Fair enough," said Ben, as he headed north at the exit while Adam recounted his last five days in Tucson, in particular the mystery surrounding the disappearance of Tyler.

Pulling up at Adam's drive, Ben jumped out of the car to retrieve the luggage from the trunk. "Don't lose too much sleep over this guy, Adam. It was a moment in time. Maybe you need to let it go now." Ben was unloading Adam's carefully crated bicycle, which would likely sit crated now until the spring.

Knowing there was no way in hell he would let that happen, Adam nodded and mumbled, "Sure thing, Dad." Adam knew the only way to do things his way was to agree to not talk about it with his dad. Feeling useless, he watched as his father stood his luggage inside the garage.

Waving goodbye, Adam unlocked the door and stepped inside. Oddly, Adam felt out of place being back home. The hospital stay seemed to have added weeks to his time away. Compounding this was the feeling that he had so much unfinished business in Tucson. He couldn't fully grasp the impact his conversations with Marin had on him. The El Tour de Tucson ride seemed like it never happened. Tyler was front and foremost on his mind. He was troubled by some of Marin's comments and wished he'd had the chance to hear the entire story. Why the hatred for her mother? Where was her mother? Why did she think her father was discussing Tyler in whispers behind the door? What exactly did that man have in a box under his bed? Was there any truth to it, or had Marin imagined it, as her father had said to her? Why did Tyler's family vanish, and to where? Was Tyler dead or alive? Or was

Marin crazy? Perhaps she was afflicted with some sort of lingering trauma.

Marin didn't strike him as a girl who would make up such a story, nor was it likely she was a conspiracy theorist. But then again, why did he feel so certain about that? These were questions for later. Right now, he did feel the need to sleep for about a week. He needed to erase the vision of her sitting in the chair beside his hospital bed and hearing her voice as she said, *"I think if anyone wanted to do anything for me, they'd help me find out where he is. Somewhere out there is either a being or a grave. All I ask is to know what happened to him."*

Adam took off his overcoat as he headed for the thermostat, only to see that Claire had beat him to it. He spotted the foil-wrapped casserole on the counter and noted the shades had been opened, allowing the light to stream into the windows. He smiled as he put the casserole in the oven and headed for the shower. He would eat and then crawl into his bed. Everything else could wait.

Following his shower and a huge plate of chicken casserole, he yawned. It was only three o'clock in the afternoon. His internal clock was definitely off track, and all he could think of was sleep. But first he had a call to make. He tried the number again.

His wife, Sofia, was currently in Italy with her mother. Sofia's grandmother had taken ill suddenly, and with no one to look after her, Sofia accompanied her mother back to Modena. Sofia had said the plan was to stay as long as needed. The last word was that they would be home early May. This took Adam by surprise, as he had no idea they could be needed for that long. Adding to the surprise, Sofia had called to inform him that she had managed to obtain a position in the neighbouring Reggio Emilia, at one of the schools. She had heard they were in need of an ESL teacher. Fortunately, Sofia held a TEFL certificate, which would allow her to teach but in a very casual capacity. Whether or not this was legal was questionable, but it helped Sofia tremendously. It allowed her to be away from the daily monotone of caring for her grandmother and running errands for her mother, plus it allowed her the time on her own to assess her life and her relationship with Adam. This, she explained, was a good break for both of them, as things had been a bit strained for the past year.

Adam initially welcomed the idea of time apart, but hearing it would be five months, he felt a twinge of panic. The upside was that Sofia's emails were kind and optimistic, and they were now at the point where they were saying things that had been unsaid for too long. Adam eventually came to the conclusion that this time apart was perhaps not a bad thing.

There was still no answer, and the call had not been picked up by voicemail. So, Adam hung up and began composing an email. Although anxious to connect with her, he wasn't planning on telling her about his accident. Not in this way, and not while she was away.

8

DURING THE NIGHT, ADAM SHIVERED WITH COLD. FOR A
split second, he thought he was still in the Oro Valley hospital,
but the quietness of the room soon made him realize he was at
home. Turning over, he told himself he needed to get out an
extra blanket. He lay awake, considering getting up, as he had
been already sleeping for a long time. But he eventually fell
asleep again and slept soundly for the remainder of the night.

He awoke to the sound of the recycling trucks groaning
and squeaking out on the street. He didn't rush to get out
of the warmth of his bed, but chose to wait for the sound of
the furnace kicking in. When it did, he slowly raised himself
onto his elbows. He knew it would take a while before he felt
himself again; the stiffness and pain were constant reminders
of his fall in the mountains.

While waiting for the kettle to boil, he called his office. He
had gazed at his reflection in the mirror and was grateful this
was only a telephone and not a video call. When his medical
assistant answered, he shut the kettle off again, knowing he'd
be a while.

A soft voice began speaking on the end of the line. "Good
morning, Doctors Jones and Wyner, how can I help you?"

"Hi, Anya, it's me, Dr. Wyner. How are things going?"

"Dr. Wyner! Welcome back! We were worried about you. Are you okay now?" she blurted, with hardly a pause between sentences. A charming woman, Anya had been with them since before Adam had joined the practice. Anya had just the right blend of compassion and practicality, mixed with a good dose of business sense, and both doctors found her invaluable.

Adam was a clinical psychologist. Clinical psychologists like him help kids cope with stresses like divorce, death, and life transitions. His patients included young adults but mostly teens with a variety of issues, from learning disabilities to severe mental illness. A partial list of problems he treated included attention deficit disorder, autism, obsessive-compulsive disorder, phobias, traumas, and adjustment disorders.

Neither Ben nor Claire was surprised when Adam chose this field, having gone through issues himself while growing up. And since he had always been a nurturer, it was a good fit and it made him happy. Adam had immersed himself into his studies at two universities and had advanced through his BA and MA with apparent ease, loving his decision more and more along the way.

Adam spent the next fifteen minutes catching up with the goings-on at his shared practice. His partner, Greg Jones, was twelve years his senior and had already been well established when Adam came aboard. They spent little time together, but the practice ran smoothly. They were like trapeze artists, coming and going at just the right time, their rhythm down to a fine art. They had each other's backs.

Once Anya had finished with the updates, Adam asked her to email his schedule of appointments for next week. He let her know he'd see her next week, then, hanging up the phone, he turned back to the kettle.

Adam was in his home office catching up on emails when his phone pinged. Looking at the screen, he saw it was a text from Nigel in England. Nigel was Claire's nephew. Claire's brother, Paul, had moved to England after marrying a British girl whom he had met here in Canada. Ever since Adam was a small boy, Ben and Claire had taken him on visits to England. Over the years, he had come to love road biking, enjoying the Derbyshire roads riding with his cousin. He read Nigel's message.

"I hear you've had a fall. Have you forgotten how to walk? Hope you're okay. Have a safe trip home. Want to tell you we have a bun in the oven. Well, Susan actually has the bun. Due in August. Call me. Nige."

This was good news, he thought, and he would call Nigel later, once he finished replying to the mound of work-related emails that had piled up. Sofia would be happy to hear this news, although it would mean additional pressure on Adam, who remained unsure about starting a family.

* * * *

THE NEXT FEW WEEKS PASSED quickly. It always amazed Adam how little time it took to fall back into a routine, as if he'd never been away. Arizona was now a blur, except for lingering body aches and the occasional thought of Tyler. He recalled Marin's conversations with greater diligence and concern. It didn't sound right, for someone to effectively disappear, unless of course he wanted to. He did want to help and was still trying to formulate a plan in his head. It's the actual plan he was struggling with, but he would act on it as soon as he had one.

On this particular Saturday morning, Adam crawled out of bed while it was still dark. He was eagerly anticipating his long overdue drive to Hamilton. His closest friend Pete lived there, in the Beasley district, and for the past four years, the two of them had been involved in brewing beer, not so much for the cost savings, but rather to learn how processes and ingredients can make a difference not only in creating different flavours and aromas, but also for the simple reason that good ingredients matter. Plus it was a good hobby for Pete.

Adam had been slow to acquire a taste for one of the oldest and most widely consumed beverages, and his appreciation had grown in part to the extensive variety from which to choose. His palate was still adjusting, but for him, it wasn't an expanding repertoire, but more shifting his taste from one blend to another, at times in rapid succession.

As was usual, Adam planned to leave early, at five, to avoid traffic. While the sun was not yet up, it was expected to be a beautiful sunny morning. There had been clear skies for the past few days, so the roads were dry. He made good time and unusually, he found he enjoyed the drive. Parking the car, he realized how much he had been looking forward to this day. Pete was grounding, and today Adam could use some solid ground under his feet.

Walking into the dimly lit brewery, he was greeted by the owner with a sideways nod in the direction of the back room. There, he found Pete, jotting down notes on the clipboard. Pete looked up and greeted his friend with a smile. He was wearing his usual faded jeans, Banana Republic sweatshirt, and bright white Pumas. Adam had often suspected that Pete had a closet full of the same outfit. The music was turned up loud, the atmosphere in the small brewery vibrant. After slapping each other warmly on their shoulders, they started talking about beer and bottling dates.

Once done, they made arrangements with the proprietor to come back and bottle this batch. Leaving the brewery, they made their way down the street to which was questionably the worst restaurant in all of Southern Ontario, but neither cared. It seemed to have become their place to go whenever they came to this part of town. It sufficed for a glass of beer and a sandwich.

Pete had been Adam's friend since his last two years at high school. They enjoyed a lot of the same school clubs, neither of them being big on the organized sports teams. For a few years, they had dated sisters, one of whom they had met at the Debate Club. After they graduated from college, Pete married his girlfriend, Linda, whereas Adam and Dana split, Adam going to university to earn the first of his degrees in psychology and Dana moving to Ottawa.

Pete was a stand out guy—the kind of friend whom you could always rely on. He was a good son to his parents and a dependable husband to Linda, as well as being one of the funniest people Adam knew. Adam had always appreciated him as a friend and a human being. Between bites of their lunch, they talked fervently, paying little attention to what they were eating, consumed more with catching up after nearly a month's lapse of seeing each other.

"You look like you've lost weight. Don't tell me I'm wrong," said Pete, scrutinizing Adam with his eagle eye.

Adam answered with a laugh. "Believe me, I've been making up for it the past three days." He eyed his burger cautiously and then carried on eating it. Adam had been extremely talkative in telling Pete about his cycling trip. "But yeah well, between the riding, the heat, and the accident, I didn't have much of an appetite."

Staring at Adam, Pete responded jokingly, "Well, judging by the way you are attacking that sandwich, I'd say you are you are on your way to recovery."

Adam hadn't realized how badly he needed to talk about the trip with his friend. Sitting here now, listening to himself say the words, he felt newly impacted by his fall. The story would have been much different and may have ended badly were it not for Marin's presence. Also, the story of Marin and Tyler sounded different to him now. It really was an odd thing, to lose track of someone in such a fashion. Adam finished his story with his current state of mind. He was curious to know more but felt he had hit a brick wall, not knowing how to find Tyler.

"So, what exactly do you want to do? I'm not sure I understand."

"Marin said something strange, and I was hoping to see her again to ask her about it. She said she had overheard her dad talking to someone on the phone and she heard Tyler's name mentioned. When she asked her dad about it, he denied it. She said her dad had been speaking about him as if he were alive. Again, her father denied it and said she was hearing things. So, I'm curious to see where the family went and to find out if by chance he is still alive. I think she'd like closure, to know where his body is, so she could say goodbye. She may be suffering from some survivor's guilt, feeling the accident was her fault."

Once they had paid the bill, they stood to leave. Walking out into the winter air, Adam wrapped his scarf tightly around his neck. He was not yet accustomed to the cold. It was a beautiful day, bright and sunny. The bright blue of the sky stood a sharp contrast against the blinding white of the snow on the rooftops. The cars on the road carried the familiar clumps of sludgy brown snow stuck to the wheel wells behind the tires. As a boy he would love to walk home from school kicking these clumps from all the cars parked along the road. But the enjoyment of those days was long gone and now it all looked perfectly disgusting. This was the worst part of winter.

Pete had carried the conversation outdoors with them. "I wouldn't even know how to begin with something like that. Particularly—or haven't you noticed—you are in Canada and she is in the US. And is there any valid or logical cause for concern? I realize it's your profession tugging at you, this survivor's guilt angle, but don't you have enough patients already?"

"Sofia is gone, Pete. I will go crazy without her, being left with so much time on my hands. This might be a good diversion to find out if the guy is dead or alive. I know it might sound dumb, but she said Tyler's dad scared her. Scared them both. So, I'd like to do this partly out of curiosity and partly as a concerned doctor."

Pete shook his head. "Still, doesn't mean there's anything behind it. Besides, how will you possibly do any record searching? Unless, of course, you happen to know any private eyes," said Pete with a grin, revealing his slightly crooked front tooth.

Adam had often referred to his friend as "Practical Pete."

He always had the shortest, most efficient answer to everything. His were logical and useful responses. He wasn't one to overthink things. Furthermore, his solutions were usually good ones. But Adam wasn't feeling too concurring this day.

They reached the corner where they would part company when Adam stopped in his tracks. "Hey, wait a minute, I do know one! Well, I don't, but my cousin Nigel does. His fiancé, Susan—Nigel said her dad, Joe Parrott, is a private eye."

"But isn't he in England? What good is that? So now you've got Canada, US, and England involved in this scheme?" Pete looked to the sky, throwing his hands up in the air, and groaned. "I think Sofia needs to come home."

Ignoring the gesture, Adam continued, "I also seem to recall something about a relative. Joe's family is originally from America. Actually, I believe he was born there. I think he still has relatives in Washington. His uncle is a cop or something like that. No wait—his cousin is a private eye. I'll have to ask Claire. Thanks, Pete. I think I'll invite myself home for dinner next week," said Adam with an enormous smile.

9

MARIN WOKE WITH A START. SHE'D HAD THAT DREAM again. She put it down to having spent all that time talking to Adam about events from the past. Wanting to release those thoughts, she stretched, long and luxuriously, like a cat. She was feeling decidedly well rested this morning. Marin anticipated that today would be a good day. Her news story on the bear attacks had been very well received, ending the week on a good note. The enticing smell of coffee was wafting in through her open window. The aroma of caffeine motivated her to jump out of bed and head straight for the shower.

Marin's roommate, Stella, had been gone for over a month, and it was becoming too often an occurrence that Marin felt she lived alone. At first, she enjoyed the freedom while trying to adjust to her new life in Arizona, but lately, she was feeling the need for the company of a roommate. Stella worked for the cruise line industry as a sous chef, and her past three cruises had been long hauls: one to Australia and two had been world cruises.

Stella had then found herself a boyfriend, who was on the same ship, so theirs was the ideal situation. It began ideal for Marin as well, as she had plenty of time to herself to deal with her lingering symptoms. While she was much better, there were still the little things. Like the nights she was afraid to turn the lights out in the hallway. And the time she dropped her mug on the floor, sending shards of porcelain flying in all directions. She had cried hysterically and not left the house for half the day until she could compose herself.

Today was Sunday, and it was gearing up to be a good day. Marin had a date with her friend Penelope. Her closest friend had invited her on a day trip to Tubac, very near the Mexican border, to an art festival. Penelope was picking her up at nine thirty, so Marin had an hour before she had to be ready. She was looking forward to the trip and the chance to get away from her daily surroundings.

The historic Presidio community of Tubac likely had a population of less than one thousand, but it was seeped in both art and history. The downtown area consisted of original old buildings mixed with newer ones. Marin guessed there were a hundred galleries, studios, restaurants, gift, and clothing shops, not to mention the metal art and endless pottery. This was only her third time to the artisan community, and she was glad that Penny had invited her.

Like clockwork, Penny's car pulled up to the curb at precisely nine thirty, where Marin stood waiting. Her friend was dressed all in white, her short blond hair blown wild from the open car window. She leaned over and gave Marin a one-arm hug, as Marin stowed her purse and water bottle by her feet and buckled up. Within seconds, Penny had pulled away from the curb and was doing a U-turn to head towards Interstate 10.

Eventually, Penelope looked over at her. "No offence, Marin, but . . ."

"Don't do that," shot back Marin.

"Don't do what?"

"Don't start a sentence like that when we both know what you are going to say will likely offend me."

Penelope's expression softened. "Okay, sorry, but what gives? You have seemed distracted lately. You've been withdrawing back into yourself again."

Marin let out a huge sigh. "It's not Tyler this time, honest. I just feel like I missed out on something big by not seeing that guy again. The one from Romero Pools."

Penelope turned down the volume before saying, "I still don't quite understand your obsession with this guy. So, what is it? Do you, like, have the hots for him or something?"

"No, no, it's nothing like that at all. It was more than that. It was a real connect, you know? It was so easy to bare it all and I couldn't stop talking. It was easier talking to him than it is to my therapist. It felt so liberating . . . satisfying. I felt like I knew him. And it seemed easy for him as well. You know, he was even finishing my sentences! We really clicked."

"Okay, so you clicked. It was nice knowing him. We meet people like that all the time. A waiter in a restaurant, the man who cleans the community center pool, the lady at the spa who pretends to be your best friend so you'll give her a big tip—we can't hang on to all of them because we think there's a connection."

"That's exactly why I don't want to talk about it, Penny. It was different. Let's leave it at that. I don't want anyone to try to convince me that it was less. That's what my mother always did, when she was still alive." Marin leaned forward and turned the volume back up. Unoffended, Penny patted Marin on the arm and drove on. She was well aware of what Marin had been through and would offer her nothing but support.

Normally, Marin spent her Sundays out on the open road. She would create a new or favourite destination each Friday. Usually, she went on these drives alone, but there had been the occasion where Penny came along. Marin's take was that Penny dared not suggest a destination but would wait to see where she had made up her mind to go. Only then would her friend decide if that would suit her. More often than not, it didn't. But this was a pleasant change. She loved that they were doing this today and wondered why she didn't come more often.

They arrived in Tubac in time to get a good parking spot. Once the car was parked and their personal belongings safely stowed in the trunk, they began their exploration of the exhibits. They wandered leisurely from shop to shop, booth to booth. Penny was an art collector and these excursions were meaningful to her, whereas Marin simply enjoyed the sights, sounds, and smells of the place. The sound of music caused them to turn their heads. A mariachi band was playing at the end of the lane, on the corner at the edge of the old barrio. An older couple had wandered over from an open-air diner and was now engaged in some sort of dance, clapping one hand against their leg while balancing their margaritas in the air with the other. Marin and Penelope stood watching for a time, enjoying their antics and sharing in the laughter.

After wandering through an exquisite woodcraft furniture shop, they meandered towards Old Tubac, along Calle Iglesia, to Marin's favourite shop, La Paloma. This particular store was not so much Mexican as it was Peruvian, with folk art from

Latin American countries like Peru, Guatemala and Ecuador. Walking into the store, the music instantly conjured up images of Machu Picchu and Santiago. Marin hummed to herself as she wandered through the rooms. After examining a few small pottery pieces, she settled on a small red and gold Talavera pottery bowl to add to her modest collection. Unexpectedly, she felt a push behind her. Penelope was tugging at her sleeve as she leaned over to whisper.

"Are you done yet? Let's go to Elvira's. I'm getting hungry."

Marin nodded in agreement. Elvira's was one of the best reasons to come to Tubac, and any shopping day wouldn't be complete without a visit to the very popular restaurant. The timing was good, as it was turning out to be quite a hot day, and Marin was feeling parched. The breeze was kicking up the dust along the unpaved streets as she followed Penelope back towards the restaurant.

They stopped at the car to put their purchases in the trunk, and just as they turned to walk on, Marin heard someone call out her name. Turning, she tensed when she saw Josh, standing across the street and waving. While not someone she was well acquainted with, he did work at the same newspaper. He looked both ways and ran across the road to where they stood.

"Oh, hi, Josh," Marin said, not meaning to sound quite so aloof. She turned to introduce her friend. "I think you've met Penny before."

"Hi, Penny. Great festival, isn't it? It's nice to see you two here. Where are you headed? Can I walk with you guys?"

"Actually, sorry, but we've got lunch plans right now, but it was nice seeing you, too, Josh." She grabbed Penelope's sleeve and led her away hurriedly.

"What was that all about?" asked a bewildered Penny.

"It's Josh, from the paper. He's always running over every time he sees me."

"But he seems really nice, and I think he likes you, Marin."

"Yeah, I got that, too. But I don't like him and I don't want to lead him on. I find him off-putting, to tell you the truth. I think he's lonely and he gets a little overbearing. Not only with me, I've seen him do it with other girls at the office. I think he's hoping for anyone to take him up on it, not necessarily me."

"But this is great! This is what you need, to put yourself out there and meet people. Maybe even date once in a while."

"But why do I need to date? I know plenty of people now. I meet lots in my line of work. I am not interested in dating anyone at this point in my life."

"But it might be good for you to get out there and fall in love or something."

"I love you, but I don't want to make myself try to fall in love with someone. We don't just go shopping and pick whom we will love; it's bigger than that. This isn't a produce store and I'm not squeezing avocadoes looking for just the right one."

"Yes, I know, but it's fun. You might find you have things in common," said Penny, trying to coax her friend. "You should be in love and not alone. You know, a little personal contact? Touching, kissing, and all that?"

"Yuck, Penny. Please don't make me sound like a prude, but love isn't a choice, or a necessity. It should be serendipitous. It's not something we can control. Besides, I'm not ready. I get by just fine, Penny. I like my life and my friends. Millions of people are single and happy! And I don't much feel like kissing." She squeezed Penny's arm gently. "Now please, let's go eat."

Marin had only been to this restaurant a few times, but each time she walked in the door she was somehow unprepared for the décor. The blown glass was startlingly mind popping. Colourful glass beads hung from the entire ceiling, from the walls, huge glass flowers were sticking out of urns – it was everywhere. True, it was original, but for Marin it was almost overkill. She felt it created nervous energy rather than calm, but then again, she was sure that's exactly what the owners wanted. Such energy could only invite thirst and appetite.

They ordered margaritas, tacos, and quesadillas and spent the next hour engaged in laughter and stupidity. Unlike Marin, Penny was no stranger to dating and was sharing funny stories of her latest boyfriend. After lunch, they walked around long enough to stave off the effects of the drink before they got into the car and headed back to Oro Valley. It had been a good day.

"Thanks for inviting me, Penny. It's been a great day." The radio was on and Penny was tapping her fingers on the steering wheel, singing along with Linda Ronstadt. Still feeling the effects of the alcohol and the heat, Marin closed her eyes and drifted into that space between sleep and awake.

Marin woke when she felt the car slow down. They had reached the outskirts of Tucson. She welcomed the breeze coming through the partly open window as she reflected on the day. Her thoughts eventually returned to Adam. She remembered that he had been very curious about what happened to Tyler. He had looked at her long and hard when she mentioned overhearing her dad speak of him, long after his supposed death. But she didn't want to think about that. She needed to start making plans for April, when she would visit Romero Pools for Tyler's birthday. She had made up her mind that would be her last trip up. What then? Maybe she'd get a puppy. Maybe she'd move further away, like New York or somewhere different, to make a fresh start. Maybe she would find a religion, or enter a convent. Or maybe . . .

Stopping the car in front of Marin's door, Penelope left the engine idling as she jumped out of the car to open the trunk. There were many bags, but only one small bag belonged to Marin—her little Talavera pot. After hugging her friend warmly, she waved goodbye and ran up the front steps.

Since Marin had moved to Oro Valley, she sometimes felt bad for avoiding her father. Her mother was gone, and she would never admit out loud just how unburdened she felt about that. Marin almost felt like a bad person that the death of her mother had only brought feelings of relief. Looking back, she felt she never could have lived up to what her mother had wanted her to be. Well, that wasn't exactly true. The truth was her mother seemed to have no expectations of Marin. There was no encouragement, no guidance, not even a hint of what she should do. Since the day Marin could get herself to school and back, her mom figured her job was done. Marin didn't want to think about that, either.

Carefully unwrapping her treasure, she made her way into her room to place the little pot on the shelf with the other three. A small collection and perhaps not very useful, but she loved the look and feel of them. They made her happy and comforted her.

Marin knew she was denying some of her emotions. But she did miss her dad, and mostly her sister. She and Lauren seldom spoke, her sister thinking she was wrong to avoid whatever family they had left and couldn't understand why Marin was punishing their dad. And what exactly was the reason behind this ostracism? But Marin felt her dad was keeping something from her, and he had been more than happy when she announced she was moving to take this job. Hell, he had practically packed her bags for her.

10

CLAIRE WAS POURING THE WINE WHEN ADAM CAME IN THE door. Soft jazzy music could be heard from the next room, and there were good smells coming from the kitchen. She walked over to greet him as he took off his coat. Hanging it up, he breathed into his hands and vigorously rubbed them together. Adam then hugged her warmly, his lips brushing her cheek. He had many fond memories of this place, which had been bought when his dad married Claire. This large brick house was on the outskirts of town, closer to Aurora than to Newmarket, and Adam had a fabulous bedroom overlooking the yard and pastures beyond. He had helped his dad build climbing apparatus in the back, and the three of them had spent many summers having backyard picnics and climbing competitions, seeing who could be the best contortionist.

When Adam had left home for university, the climbing apparatus had been replaced with a few trees, a gazebo, and a fire pit table, much more in line now with a childless home. Sofia's heart had sunk when the play area was dismantled, as she had hoped her and Adam's own children would be able to use it. Adam knew he needed to have that conversation with his wife when she returned from Italy. Looking out the kitchen window into the yard, he envisioned it in the summer and not as it was now, buried under a blanket of shimmering snow and ice, looking frigidly uninviting.

"You look better," Claire said, giving him the thumbs up as she sat down.

"I am starting to feel better." He rolled his shoulders back and took a deep breath. "Thanks so much for this dinner, Claire. Where's Dad?" he asked, glancing down the hallway.

"You're early. He's not back yet. He went for a run with Kate."

Kate DeLucci was Claire's best friend and former room-mate. She and Claire had met at the wedding of Claire's brother, Paul. Paul and his wife, Suki, now lived in England, where Nigel was born. Kate and Paul had become good friends in school, both having been quite athletic. It wasn't until Paul's wedding that Kate had met Claire, as Claire had been away in Greece for quite some time. Shortly after Paul's departure, Kate found a house to rent and had approached Claire with the hope she'd be interested in sharing.

They had moved in together soon afterwards and had remained roommates until Claire's wedding to Ben. Although Kate had herself met someone, she was very upset when they gave up their little house and each went their separate ways. Claire had endured the death of a boyfriend and the subsequent investigation, which had put her life in danger. The entire misadventure had bonded the women even further.

Since Claire's brush with death, when she had been purposely run over by a car, Kate no longer enjoyed running alone. Her partner, Philippe, or Phil as he preferred to be called, had stopped running due to a knee injury, so for many years now,

Ben and Kate would run together, often once a week.

Claire and Paul were children of Russian immigrants and, while not always close, had become so in the years leading up to Paul's departure. Adam had often heard Claire tell his dad how much she missed her brother. Adam had only met Nigel a dozen times or so, but they got along well and enjoyed cycling together. Nigel was quick to share the news with his step-cousin when he met Susan, the girl of his dreams. He had fallen in love with her quite quickly. Now Adam needed to have a word with Nigel, but not before first discussing it with Claire and his dad.

Claire motioned to a chair. "Sit down, Adam. You do look tired and you seem to have a lot on your mind. Have you spoken with Sofia lately? Oh—and how is your leg? You aren't limping anymore, I see."

Adam sat down and accepted the glass of wine that Claire had poured for him. He filled her in on the latest news with Sofia. Then wasting no more time, he blurted out, "Didn't Nigel say that Susan's father, Joe, is a private eye? And didn't he have a cousin who is the same, in Washington?"

"Uh-oh," said Claire. "His name is Steve and what are you up to, Adam? Is this about the girl in Arizona who helped you?"

"It's a long shot, I know, but just what if he could help me to uncover something? You see, it all fits together, like perfect puzzle pieces. Marin says she comes from Washington, and that's where she and her boyfriend had the accident. If Steve lives in the area, it might be easy for him to check it out."

Claire let out a little laugh. "I know what you mean about wanting to know—our curiosity can get the better of us. But I'm not sure you should tell your dad. He wasn't too happy when I played detective. It clashed with his sensibilities and his cautiousness. Besides, I don't think you're cut out for this."

"Yes, but from what I heard you were dealing with a dead body and a few subsequent deaths. You were caught in the middle of murders and all that stuff, from what I was told. We never know what we are cut out for." Adam smiled at her before adding, "Besides, you're a girl."

Claire's eyes flashed a warning. She was still very beautiful, and her eyes had not lost their magnetism. "Who are you calling a girl?"

In defense, Adam exclaimed, "But you are a girl! I'm not trying to sound sexist, but Dad would have worried about you getting hurt. Which, by the way, you did get hurt! Didn't someone run you over with a car?"

Claire sat back in her chair, recalling the mysterious death of her then-lover, Will. "Yes, well, aside from that." She thought for a moment then added, "Do you know, I was a year younger than you are now when I went through that. It was hard on your father."

"Circumstances are very different though, aren't they?"

"Yes, I agree, they are very different. All you want is to find a missing person. Or at least some confirmation of life or death." She crossed her legs and looked at Adam with a new seriousness. She was studying his face. He did look tired, and at this moment, he looked alarmingly like his father. "This girl has really gotten to you, hasn't she?"

In the distance a train's whistle blew, like an old familiar friend. It seemed no matter where you lived in town the sound of the whistle could be heard. Adam glanced up at the window. The forlorn wail and the faint clickety clack of the tracks that often rocked him to sleep when he was young sounded crisp and clear, even through the closed window. He tried to remember the song that Claire would sing to him when he couldn't sleep.

Adam looked at the floor, then back at Claire. He took his time answering. "I don't know which has gotten to me more. I'd sure like to know what happened to him. If he's alive, I hope that he's safe. Do you know what she said to me? She said he was the best thing that ever happened to her and she didn't want to die thinking she was the worse thing that ever happened to him." Adam shifted uncomfortably in his seat. He hesitated as if deciding whether or not to continue. He looked up but not directly at Claire. "Do you remember when I was about eleven or twelve, there was that boy that went missing somewhere near Kitchener? His mother and father were frantic. The kid just disappeared. The police were on the news every day, and it scared the shit out of me. After five or six months, everybody stopped looking. They just got on with their lives. But I was traumatized. I had nightmares and I couldn't sleep. I couldn't believe that that could happen. Then three years later, they found the boy in a neighbour's cellar, covered in sores and half dead. And for the next year, everyone was on about how they should have done more. The mother had a breakdown and was never the same again. And the words that echoed through the air were, *'we should have done more, we should have kept looking.'* Did you know that statistics say there are about three hundred kids missing in Ontario right now? Some have been missing since the forties. What if something went wrong?

Claire looked at Adam, helpless. She didn't know what to say. "Like what?" she mustered.

Adam answered, "Okay, for starters, where's the grave?"

Just then the door opened. His dad was home.

* * * *

AFTER SUPPER, THE THREE OF them retired to the sofa by the fireplace. Adam was determined to have this conversation with them. He turned to Ben and Claire and added, "There must have been a reason why I fell in front of her. And to be honest, I am more than curious myself. She was an unusual girl. Some big things happened in her short life—major things. She seemed happy enough, but there was definitely an underlying affliction. Just maybe I was meant to find Tyler."

Ben looked at his son and said, "Is this where you give me this whole fate and destiny thing?"

Adam smiled at his dad and said, "But I don't have any answers. Whatever your philosophy, and what you believe, there could be a reason why we met. Whether you believe Kierkegaard or Aristotle, I think the meaning is all the same. Or if you believe in Buddhism and karma, however you want to look at it, Marin and I did present our selves to each other. If it was Marin's fate to end up living in Arizona, recovering emotionally and physically, was it destiny that I fell in front of her? Or was it just a coincidence? I'm a realist, not a fatalist. I fell in front of her for a reason."

"Do you really believe that, son?"

"Yes, Dad, I do. She's fighting to get her life back on track. And maybe I can help her find some closure."

Claire squeezed his hand gently. "It's all about trust. Do you trust your instincts? Do you trust what she said to you?"

Adam smiled at her. "Yes, I do."

Claire looked at Ben, then smiled back at Adam and said decisively, "I will let Nigel and Susan know that they can expect a call from you."

11

ADAM WAS UNSURE WHETHER TO CALL NIGEL OR SEND HIM a message. He decided on the message, as it would allow the best opportunity to explain what it is he wanted. He was unsure how much Claire would have told them. Adam wouldn't push to speak with Susan's father, Joe - he would leave that up to Nigel. He was really only concerned with the guy in Washington. He composed a brief summary of the issue and sent it off, holding his breath. Now, he just needed to wait for a reply.

In the meantime, he found himself doing web searches about car accidents, but he got nowhere. What did he expect? He couldn't even remember the girl's last name, if she even told him. All he had was two first names, hers and Tyler's. Yes, but Tyler what? He searched their first names together and got nothing. Then he tried to remember the soccer club that Tyler had been accepted to. That part wasn't difficult, as he did remember it was the Portland Timbers. So, he expanded his search to the team, searching for any of the members being involved in a near-fatal crash. Or was it fatal? His search brought up nothing, as he didn't know the date. And for that matter, Tyler wasn't an actual team member yet.

Over the next few weeks, he persevered. He would do a few searches a day, using different words, different phrases. He always came up empty and feeling more frustrated. Just when he felt like pulling his hair out, he would find diversions, such as his very important medical practice. It bothered him a bit that he wasn't giving it quite the required attention. He needed to smarten up.

Then one day, his phone pinged. It was Nigel saying that he had contact information for Joe's cousin Steve Henderson, in Seattle. Adam was beside himself. This was extremely good news. He hardly read the message when he switched on his phone and dialed Nigel's number.

"Hallo?" said the familiar voice on the other end of the line.

"Nige, it's me. I just had to call you. This is really great news, thank you. I owe you a beer."

"Don't thank me yet, Adam. I don't know what Steve will say. I talked to Joe and told him your story, and he sent a few messages to Steve before he heard back. Steve is Joe's sister's son and they have never been close, so he wasn't sure he would receive a response. But then he did receive two messages. Steve said you could contact him, but he would make no promises about what he could do for you."

"No, this is good. If it works, it works. If not, so be it. I just know I'll feel a lot better if I just try." Adam had seated himself in the kitchen, on his favourite stool at the island.

"This girl's got to you then, Adam?" Nigel's voice lowered slightly. "Do you fancy her or something?"

"No, Nige, it's really not like that. I mean yes, I like her in a friend way, in a kindred way. She did help me, maybe more than I realize. I was wearing thin hiking trousers and a T-shirt, and the temperature at night can dip below freezing in the mountains in November. And to top it off, I had blood on me. While lying there crippled and dazed, I could easily have been attacked by a cougar. I'm lucky she was there. She's young, and I believe she's hurting; she's lost something big. She did an amazing thing for me, and it could be a great ending if I can help her, too."

"Or not," warned Nigel, thinking of Susan's dad, Joe, and the case that just recently blindsided him. "Things don't always turn out the way we hope. And we can be fooled about who people really are."

"Yes, so I've heard," said Adam, himself thinking of Claire. "But if it starts to go sour, I'll stop. I just need to try."

They spoke for a bit longer, talking about Nigel's veterinarian practice, which had really taken off. Then the conversation finally landed on Susan and the unexpected pregnancy. They were both thrilled and were busy making plans for a family reunion once the baby was born. Susan would continue working at her clinic for as long as she could, wanting to save the time off for after the baby was born and Nigel's family arrived.

"Your aunt Claire is pretty excited." Adam laughed.

Nigel chortled, "I know. My dad and my aunt Claire are on the phone all the time, making their plans. So maybe I'll see you in August, right, mate? Maybe your mystery will be solved by then, and Sofia will be home."

Hanging up, Adam suddenly missed Sofia. He sat and stared at his hand and pictured hers on top of it, her small, delicate fingers interweaving into his own. He pictured the day he had put a ring on that finger. Adam had met Sofia during his first year of university. He had come home for the summer, and on that day, he was at Kensington Market with Claire. It was late Saturday morning, and the market was bustling with people. Because of the narrow streets, parking was always a challenge. People would walk freely down the middle of the road and between cars, so Adam was driving with caution.

In front of him were two women, hurrying along but walking immediately in front of his car. Up ahead, he spied a parking space and was hoping nobody would get to it before he did. But he was concentrating more on the two women in front of him. The one on the right was wearing a knee-length flowered dress and sandals, and her head was tilting back in laughter. She had shoulder-length curly hair, ebony black. She had an easy sway to her hips, her skirt flowing rhythmi-cally from side to side. The women seemed oblivious to the car behind them, and he was happy to be driving slowly in observation.

As Adam pulled in to park in the spot, which thankfully was still empty, the two women were putting their bags into the car directly in front of him. He parked quickly and jumped out to help them. The women turned, looking surprised, for they didn't think they appeared in need of help. Adam could tell right away that they were mother and daughter. Their English was elementary, and when he asked where they were from, they had said Italy. Claire had sat waiting in the car, a smile on her face. She was enjoying this immensely, Adam blubbering all over this beautiful young girl. Claire later told Adam that she had been flabbergasted when he came over to the window to announce that the two women would be having coffee with him and his mom. Claire, ever the good sport, got out of the car and, with a smile, had come over to join them.

Sofia was her name. She and her parents had immigrated to Canada only eight months previous, from Modena. Since arriving, they had spent most of their time in school, fervently studying English. Adam was quick to compliment them on their progress. Sofia's father came from a long line of balsamic vinegar producers, a condiment which dated back to the 1600s. Sofia already had a temporary job at the local community college as a teacher in the languages department, teaching, naturally, Italian.

Adam wasted no time in offering his services to show them around the area, or to be available to answer any questions or help out in any way as they settled in. He remembered the way she had smiled at him shyly, not really making eye contact. Over time, he won her heart. It was, as Marin had described with her relationship with Tyler, immediately apparent that Sofia was the one. He just knew he would never need to look again.

12

ADAM SPENT LITTLE TIME DELIBERATING BEFORE THE DECI-
sion was made to call Steve. He reread Nigel's text and
noted the man's name was Steve Henderson. The company
he worked for was American Investigators Incorporated.
Checking his watch to calculate the time difference, he
changed his mind and decided to call Monday around one in
the afternoon, when it would be ten in the morning in Seattle.
In the meantime, he did a search of the organization. He found
an abundance of companies with the same or similar names.
He came to the conclusion that not much imagination went
into naming investigative firms in the United States.

Monday came quickly. Calling as planned, he was disappointed when he heard a recorded message and not a person.
Following the prompts, he touched all the appropriate
numbers until he got to Steve's voicemail. It was a big, com-
manding voice, no-nonsense and to the point. Feeling slightly
intimidated by the sound of the man, Adam left a short message
and remembered to reference Joe Parrott. His message gave a
time that he would try calling back, not wanting the man to
feel obligated to call him in Toronto.

Adam then grabbed his coat and scarf and headed for the

door. Once he finished his appointments with patients, he would come home and try again. Adam's clinic was a thirty-minute drive from his home. He would have preferred less travel time, but as the firm had been established long before he came on board, there was no likelihood that Greg would consider relocating. Adam and Sofia had discussed moving, but they both loved where they lived and came to the conclusion that thirty minutes was nothing. He eventually had adjusted to the commute, which was only shitty this time of year and far better during the summer months.

His job, while he loved it immensely, was not always easy. Adam had real compassion for the kids he treated, and he worked hard at not carrying their burdens around with him. He often wished the parents themselves would seek treatment, as he often felt they were the real problem. But, as we all know, no license is required to become a parent. He often thought of his own mother and how smart she had been to leave. Adam couldn't help but think that he himself might have become negatively affected if she had stayed.

Once back home, before he even removed his coat, he was on the phone. It was picked up on the second ring. Adam started speaking right away.

"Mr. Henderson, it's me. Adam Wyner. I understand that your cousin Joe Parrott spoke with you about me. Thank you for agreeing to speak with me."

"How's it going, Adam? Yes, Joe called me. I guess you and me are extended family, right? Funny how one family can become so spread out. Look at us now, spanned from the West Coast to the east and overseas. It makes it easier to understand how these things happen when I have cases where

I think, 'how the hell did they get all the way over there.' Now, it makes more sense to me. Anyway, back to your problem. To tell you the truth, I was at first reluctant to help. I'd like to hear more from you, to see exactly what it is you are after. Then I'll decide. So, you want to find some girl you met in Arizona?"

"No, I know where the girl is. It's the family of her boyfriend whom I'm looking for. Their son, Tyler, was in a car accident with the girl, Marin. His family is from your area, and the accident occurred there. There's a conflicting opinion as to whether or not the guy died in the accident. I'm actually trying to find out what happened to him."

""Okay, I think I can piece together what you are saying. Well, this is not what I imagined you wanted, but I'm happy to check some things out for you. So, let's get started. Tell me what you've got."

Steve Henderson sounded all work and no play, but there was goodness in his voice. Nigel's fiancé, Susan, had nothing but love for her relatives, believing them all to be good people. And Nigel had always spoken highly of her father's humanity and congeniality, and so Adam was hopeful that Joe's cousin shared those traits.

"I'm afraid to tell you that your work will be cut out for you. That is, if you even agree to help me. The thing is, I don't know much and what I know is vague at best. I know that her name is Marin and his name is Tyler. I'm sorry, but I have no last names. I know the accident occurred roughly three years ago, but I don't know what month and I'm not a hundred percent sure of the year, but I believe it was 2012. I do know that the Portland Timbers soccer club had just accepted Tyler. And they had been to Portland that morning. I don't know if there's a specific time of year that these teams recruit new players. I think she mentioned February? She said it was cold."

"And so, what do you need from me?"

"Well, first of all, who are these kids? Who are their parents? Apparently, Tyler's dad was a big contractor, but like I said, I have no last name. There might be record of their car accident. It was apparently pretty nasty. Did Tyler survive? There appears to be some disagreement as to whether he lived or died."

"And what is this to you, if I might ask?" asked Steve.

"She saved my life, so to speak. I fell off a cliff and she helped me off the mountain. It was dark, and I don't want to think how I might have fared if she wasn't there. She told me quite the story, but there was a small part of it that didn't make sense. I believed all of what she said, but I also think she is very troubled. Both kids nearly died, from what she has said, but now, she's heard two versions of what happened to Tyler. I'm a doctor, and I can't help being concerned."

"Leave it with me, Adam. I can put out some feelers, ask some questions. But I will need to wait for answers, so I might not get back to you right away. The problem is that this is not top priority, so I don't know how quick a response I'll get from anyone. But just know I'm on it. Basically, don't call me, I'll call you, okay?"

Adam let out a big sigh of relief. "I can't ask for any more than that. I don't know how to thank you, Steve."

Business being concluded, Steve added, "So I hear your brother is marrying my cousin Joe's daughter Susan?"

"Well, my step-cousin, actually, but yes, exciting, isn't it? And a baby on the way."

"I guess it's the new way to do things. Baby first, marry later-if at all. Whatever works for people these days. I'm sorry I haven't had the chance to meet Susan yet, but I will some day. I haven't seen Joe since we were kids, but our parents still talk occasionally."

Adam concurred. "England is a long way to go. I used to see Nigel every few years but I don't think I've seen him for ten years now, so I know how you feel."

They exchanged pleasantries for a few minutes longer before Steve was ready to hang up.

"Okay, then, leave this with me. And don't thank me yet. Let's see what I can find. Talk later." And just like that, the man was gone.

13

Marin had just come in from a brisk walk on the Rillito River Loop Trail. These paved paths were part of a system known as "The Loop," which was one of the first things that she and Tyler had loved about the area. These Loop trails were built into the dirt banks along the Rillito, Santa Cruz, and Pantano rivers. When the walls had been reinforced following great floods, these access roads were built at the same time. The access roads were then paved and center lines were added, creating an amazing network of cycling and walking paths that steadily grew throughout the communities. The Loop was now about ninety percent complete, with well over a hundred miles of paved paths stretching from Oro Valley along the Cañada del Oro wash to downtown Tucson and out towards the town of Marana. Add in a few sections of city streets, and one could cycle all the way to the airport.

Aside from the fun of walking and cycling without any cars, the Loop then began connecting people to events like farmers' markets, music festivals, coffee, and lunch destinations and a way to get into the city without the hassle of traffic and parking. Along the route were public washrooms, water fountains, and even access to golf courses. This had fast become one of Marin's favourite pastimes. The desert landscape in these washes was very unique, and she never grew tired of the ruggedness.

While not too hot outside, it had been very windy. Marin was averse to windy days, as they left her feeling rattled. The wind had an unnerving aspect to it, having the ability of leaving emotional calamity in its wake. She hurried up the steps to the front door. Once inside, Marin stripped off her dusty clothes in the entrance and stuffed them under her arm as she padded through the condo on her way to the laundry room. After grabbing a tall glass of water, she headed to the bathroom. A nice bubble bath was in order.

As the tub was filling, she leaned back and closed her eyes. As hard as she tried, she couldn't stop her thoughts from wandering back to the minutes leading up to the accident. Her therapist had been working with her on exercises designed to avert these thoughts, but today, she let them happen. Marin had also been trying hard to remember things, so she always struggled with the concept of remembering while trying to forget. She shut the water off. The house was quiet, except for the fridge motor that had just kicked in.

Breathing deeply, the vision began to materialize. She was driving, and the radio was blasting. She was unable to remember the song. She knew she was drunk but didn't feel it through the euphoria of the occasion. She was laughing so hard she thought she might pee her pants. Tyler was in the passenger seat. His mouth was moving, but she couldn't hear what he was saying. He rolled his window down and spit out his gum. As he did so, a gust of cold air blasted into the car, and she remembers screaming. He turned towards her in his seat and began to tickle her.

She could almost hear his voice as her spoke to her. "What are you screaming about, sissy? Are you afraid of a little cold?" Tyler had said, teasing her. He looked up and started to say something else.

She stretched her reach to tickle back, and that was all she remembered. No, wait. She remembers him screaming and the car leaving the road, sliding. She had lost control. The car was tumbling sideways down the snowy slope. Then nothing. Had she hit something? Had something hit them? She punched her forehead with her fist. Why couldn't she remember anything else? Was there another car? What was Tyler saying to her at that moment?

The next time she opened her eyes, she was lying in a bed with tubes in her arms and down her throat. The doctors and her father told her she had been awake off and on, but she had no recollection before that exact moment. They also told her she had spoken, but she couldn't remember that either. What had she said? Her dad told her she had been here for months. He was crying. Did he say months? Marin believed she was having a bad dream, a nightmare, and that soon she would wake up. Everything moved in slow motion. Voices sounded like they were under water. And she couldn't move her legs for the longest time. All she wanted to do was sleep so that she could finally wake up at home. But each time she woke up, her panic grew as she slowly realized this wasn't a dream at all, but real life.

Her first memory of lucidity was much later. She was in a different room, with different faces around her. The nurses told Marin that she had been in something of a catatonic state for a very long time. They were very kind to her, but they looked at her funny, like she was some kind of freak. They would leave the room and whisper in the corridor. A few days passed before her father came in to see her. Her first question was, "Where is Tyler?" Then, "Where is Mom?" Her father had managed to avoid both questions, saying they would talk later. He just kept telling her to get stronger.

Marin remembered the day the doctor came to see her. He told her she had suffered a traumatic brain injury as the result of a horrendous car crash. Her consciousness level on the GCS scale was around eight, but he told her that he the scale is a measuring tool only and not necessarily a true indication of what the end result would be. The Glasgow Coma Scale (GCS), he explained, is the most common scoring system used to gauge the severity of brain injury. The test is reliable, the doctor went on the say, and correlates pretty well with outcome following severe brain injury. It is, however, not carved in stone. Each individual will have different outcomes, particularly if the scale is above seven. Marin could only nod. The doctor, she learned later, had been concerned about how much she understood.

Marin had been in a coma for some time and had been left slightly paralyzed on her right side. But it was taken as a good sign that she did know who she was and that she had been asking about Tyler and her family. She was told she would need a lot of therapy to learn how to walk, talk, get dressed, everything all over again. The doctors said she was a fighter. Her dad said she had God on her side to help her. After all, although she was only nineteen years old, she had spunk and had always displayed tenacious strength.

Then came the gut punch. Tyler was dead, as was Marin's mother. Tyler apparently didn't survive the crash, although when he was initially brought in, Marin's father was told both kids would likely survive. Tyler had been ejected from the vehicle. His injuries were substantially worse than Marin's.

But what was this about her mother? What happened to her? Surely, she had some recollection of her mother being at the hospital when she woke up in her new room. Marin was certain that she wasn't hallucinating. But again, her father was vague. "You need to get strong, Marin. We can talk later," was all he would say.

Looking back, she hadn't forgiven him for that. But now, she was changing her stance. His actions might not have been intentional, for certainly he would have had a hard time dealing with it all. Maybe he did believe she would heal better if she got strong again before being given all of the bad news. At the time, Marin felt it wasn't fair, particularly once she was capable of comprehension. But maybe she was being too hard on him. It couldn't have been easy at that time, losing his wife and worried about Marin's outcome. She needed to keep reminding herself that everyone grieves differently.

Marin had fought hard to come back. One of the lingering effects was that it left her with a bad sleeping disorder and short-term memory loss. But as she was doing now in her tub, practice was helping her memory. She was struggling less to remember things. Still, she felt things were being kept from her, like the death of her mother. She was having a problem believing her mom would take her own life. She tried hard to find some memory of her mother's behaviour in the last days leading up to the accident. Had she noticed anything different that she couldn't now remember?

Whenever she sat in this hot, comforting bubble bath, she fought back the temptation to just sink below the bubbles and make it all go away. This was exactly why her therapist never encouraged her to do this. This was not the way for her to do her remembering exercises. Not here, not in tub.

14

ADAM HAD NO PROBLEM STAYING BUSY OVER THE NEXT FEW weeks. He had eight client appointments today alone, and his calendar was full for the next few weeks. His and Greg's practice was a very busy one, and client numbers often increased in the winter. Adam's clients were children and young adults with issues such as autism, dealing with divorce, ADHD, and, in his opinion, plain old bad parenting. December was again turning out to be a busy month, with depression and anxiety always peaking at this time of year. For children who have Reactive Attachment Disorder or have experienced early childhood trauma or have been diagnosed with ADHD, the holidays can be hard. In fact, sometimes kids in those categories will sabotage Christmas, as holidays often come with sensory overload.

Personally, Christmas didn't hold much magic for Adam, regardless of how much he had enjoyed it as a child. He believed that for him the secret lay in the fact that his dad had never made a big deal of it. Adam had never attended church and was not raised with religion, so his family didn't celebrate the spiritual aspect of Christmas. But he loved the story of Christmas more than he loved the idea of Santa Clause. They visited friends and relatives, but exchanged only one gift apiece, placing far more emphasis on camaraderie, food, and games. As he grew older, he was no longer interested in gifts, as he managed to buy for himself all the things he needed during the year. As an adult, when Christmas came around, he disliked the idea of being saddled with a useless gift and also being faced with the difficult task of what to buy for family members. So over time, Christmas took on a more personal feel—a meal, a bottle of wine, and looking forward to quality time spent with family and to catch up with those friends whom he rarely saw due to busy lives.

As for his patients, they seemed less content with the idea of simplicity. Adam felt that some people placed far too much value on spending money than actually enjoying each other, and their kids often suffered, having not only their own stress to deal with but that of their parents as well. He thought it had a lot to do with parents trying to recreate their happy child-hood memories of Christmas and forcing those memories onto their kids, who were not at all interested.

This year, Adam's own Christmas would be the usual low-key, but even more so with the absence of Sofia. This only served to reinforce his notion that the magic of Christmas lay in the presence of his loved ones. Being on his own, there was no tree, although he did hang the outside lights, keeping in step with the neighbours. Sofia would have been disappointed if theirs was the only house on the block that sat in darkness. Adam now sat watching, pleased with the result. The glow of the tiny glass lights bounced off the mirror and was cast back on the walls of the room.

On Christmas Eve, Adam visited his grandparents at the nursing home in Markham. On this visit, he really noticed a decline, as his grandmother kept calling him Ben and asking him where little Adam was. His grandfather simply smiled, saying very little, making Adam unsure whether his grandfather even knew what was going on. That evening, he stayed up in front of the fire sipping brandy until the wee hours, calling his parents at midnight to say Merry Christmas, as Ben and Claire had flown to Vancouver to spend Christmas with Claire's mother.

On Christmas morning, Adam deliberately slept in. Looking out the bright, high window, he lay and watched the clouds scuttle along the uninspiring grey sky. Eventually, he did rise as the clouds slowly gave way to glimpses of blue sky. He fed himself then spent the rest of the morning showering and tidying the house, watching the clock in anticipation of his phone call with his wife.

By eleven, Adam was ready for his video chat with Sofia and her family. He had made himself a large black coffee and had laced it liberally with Baileys and Kahlúa, and he sat in front of the fire, the sun warming his feet, which were propped on the coffee table. Sofia had answered on the first ring and promptly held up a bottle to show that her coffee was laced with grappa. Her mother shook her head in feigned disapproval. It was late morning in Toronto, and early evening in Italy.

As the conversation progressed, Adam found himself telling Sofia about his mishap in Arizona. It had been well over a month ago and he had all but recovered, so he no longer felt the need to keep it from her. She had expressed a lot of support when he told her about Marin. They were similar, Adam decided. Sofia and Marin, both self-sufficient and profoundly independent and capable. Marin had been traumatized but seemed to be fighting her way back in an admirable way. Sofia agreed there was something very curious as to the fate of Tyler.

"Just be careful, whatever you do," Sofia said, her voice full of warmth.

"And with that, I think it's time to go, my love," Adam replied. "I will talk to you at New Year's. And, by the way, I won't miss the lentils and red underwear." Adam was referring to the Italian tradition that Sofia's family still continued—that of eating a meal of lentils at midnight on New Year's Eve, and of course, wearing red underwear.

That evening Adam watched *Love Actually* and *The Holiday*. These were Sofia's favourite Christmas movies, and each had agreed to watch them that evening. Part way through *The Holiday*, he switched over to *Home Alone*, then *Die Hard* before giving up on everything and turning off the television. Instead, he leaned his head back and turned on the music.

It had been a good conversation with Sofia. She looked genuinely please to be speaking with him. Her mother and even her grandmother had blown kisses. He could feel Sofia coming back, the conversation having been very loving. She had shyly giggled and looked down when he spoke, as she had back when they were dating. She also brought up the issue of starting a family and was he ready. She would be thirty this year and, as Adam was well aware, was more than ready. This time, he agreed with her, causing Sofia to smile, eyes wide open. He had been skeptical in the past, and that had a lot to do with the distance between them, but his apprehension had been slowly waning.

On the day that he and Sofia said goodbye at the airport, the cool indifference should not have come as a surprise to Adam.

The tension between them had been profoundly obvious for some time now. She had made it very clear when they met that above all else, she wanted babies. She believed that was the sole purpose of her existence on earth. Her cousin had three and she cherished them all.

And herein lay the problem. Adam had knowingly deceived her. He had always been afraid to have children, in part having been abandoned by his mother, but also because of his work. The number of messed up kids that he dealt with each week, month, year, frightened him. Adam had watched intelligent, educated parents struggle and wonder how it all went wrong. Sitting there alone in the dark, the same fears still lingered. Would he be capable of avoiding these issues with his own children? Could anyone give him guarantees? Sofia had been shattered when his repeated excuses suddenly became clear to her. He at last admitted he was afraid to have children.

The next morning, Adam bundled up to go for a walk outside. For him, walking in the fresh air was a good way to think. He and Sofia often took long walks when they had issues to discuss and found that by the time they returned from their walk, most issues had been resolved. Except for one. Adam was not ready to start a family, and Sofia ached for one. Although her trip to Italy had not been planned, it did allow them the space needed from one another to better see the situation. So, although Sofia had not changed her stance, Adam was now beginning to move over to her side.

Walking down the cold icy street, he kept warm with images of the Arizona desert. He loved the transition from blue sky and blazing sun to the intense golden sunsets in a sky that instantly darkened to black. Thinking of Arizona, Adam's mind wandered back to Marin. He deduced she had good friends based on their conversations, but he thought about whether or not she would travel to Washington to visit her family. He never did discover the status between her and her parents. She had been very vocal about disliking her mother. Adam had a plan to contact the Search and Rescue people to see if they had logged the callout on the evening of his fall. Surely, they would have record of Marin, not just her name but perhaps possibly her number. He smiled at himself, pleased that he came up with that idea. Claire might be impressed, as she had doubted his sleuthing abilities. He would run it by her when she returned from her holiday.

Adam was not a big fan of outdoor winter activities. He would have preferred to be in Arizona himself, riding his bike or hiking in the mountains. But in the meantime, he preferred indoor pursuits, like making beer, watching TV, catching up on office work, and drinking wine with Pete. He and Pete would soon be making their plans to go to the Niagara Ice Wine festival. This was his biggest winter thrill, marking the end of all the Christmas madness. Also, he had a project that he was working on, something for Sofia.

For the past few months, Adam had been busily involved in refinishing a piece of furniture for his wife. This particular piece was a French Provencal chest of drawers that they had picked up at a second-hand store in Unionville. Although not certain it was an antique, Sofia had wanted it so badly, even though Adam thought it looked terrible, given the sickly shade of paint. She loved it because it was the perfect size, having only six drawers rather than the usual nine. Sofia had never said so, but she had always hoped that Adam would refinish it for her. Over the years, he had become quite good at furniture finishing.

Now that the stripping was almost done, he wanted to be sure he correctly prepared the wood before either painting or staining. Yesterday, upon the recommendation from one of his friends, Adam had contacted a finisher who had offered to show Adam some of his works in progress and guide him through techniques and materials. So, Adam had driven to Holland Landing to visit the operation. He had taken Yonge Street, turning left on Eagle Street in order to drive past what was once the home of Claire's grandparents. He continued along Eagle but rather than turn left on Main Street, he carried on across the Water Street bridge to have a look at Fairy Lake Park.

He remembered reading about the devastating Hurricane Hazel that had swept through this town in 1954, washing out this bridge. Adam wondered if the street had been named Water Street after that day, when the Holland River had flooded it's banks and wiped out the original wooden bridge that spanned the area from the foot of Main Street to Cotter Street. Overlooking the area is the York Region Police Department. At that location, there once stood a historic building, which housed Office Specialty Manufacturing, a major industry in the town for over seventy-five years.

Adam had turned in to Fairy Lake Park, amazed at how everything had changed. It had been his first time back to the area in a very long time. He had driven slowly to the turn around area, and in his mind, he had envisioned himself as a boy, running after the geese and laughing. Claire and his dad had always packed a small picnic, and Adam had fed the leftover bread to the ducks and swans. Being there again, he had imagined how nice it would be for he and Sofia to bring their own child here and do the same.

Exiting the park, Adam had then headed up Main Street. The street had changed dramatically since he was a teen. Most of the old shops were gone, but somehow the street had not lost his charm. He noticed the addition of eating establishments, now with outdoor seating. He vowed to come back soon and walk either side, exploring as if for the first time.

Returning from his walk, Adam had attacked the project with new enthusiasm, and the day had passed quickly. He had just removed all of the old finish, which was a hideous shade of green, a blend of olive and mint. He was able to remove most of the finish with sandpaper, but the entire front of the piece had needed a chemical stripper to be applied. Now, he stood back and admired the completely stripped dresser. It looked vastly improved, even if it were to be left bare. This, he hoped, would be a comely surprise for Sofia when she arrived, as he hoped to have it in place in their bedroom.

Wiping his hands with one of his rags, Adam checked his watch. In doing so, he caught a whiff of himself. The grimy cloth had done little to remove the stench of wood finishing chemicals from his flesh. The time was later than he realized, so he quickly tidied up his workspace. Tonight, he had dinner plans with Pete and his wife, Linda. After taking a very long shower to get rid of all the wood dust, he dressed quickly, choosing a grey sweater and jeans. Grabbing his keys, he headed out he door.

Adam warmed the car up for a few minutes before backing out of the drive. He slowly headed out of his neighbourhood

Romero Pools

and towards the highway. It wasn't a long drive to the steakhouse in Rexdale, and traffic was light. He brought his car to a halt a few feet from the door, where a valet offered to park the car. He didn't say no, as it was a terrible evening, with gusty winds and sub-zero temperatures. He was the first to arrive, and so he sat in the lounge, in one of two big easy chairs by the fireplace. The hostess brought him a glass of red wine, just as Linda came into the building. He stood when he saw her enter and greeted her with a peck on the cheek.

"Pete is parking the car," she said demurely.

Linda was a charming person, but she wasn't one for big conversation. She had remained perpetually shy her whole life. It made her seem helpless and vulnerable, but she was far from that. She had a good head on her shoulders and had a strong sense of right from wrong. Adam offered his easy chair, and she sat down. There was a table between the two chairs. Adam set his drink down but remained standing, watching the door for Pete. Adam leaned forward to say something to Linda, but before he could say more than a few words, Pete came in the door, bringing a gust of wind with him. Linda stood up and smiled warmly at the two men as the hostess came to escort them to their table. Adam felt relaxed and happy and was looking forward to a good evening with his old friends.

15

MARIN WAS IN THE BATHROOM PUTTING ON THE FINAL touches of her makeup. She was not looking forward to the company Christmas party, but she was hoping she'd have a good time once she got there. It was a warm evening, despite being mid-December. She had never been to the Hilton El Conquistador before and admittedly was excited about the venue. She was told there would be a magnificent sunset around the time the party was to start, so she planned on arriving a few minutes early.

Pulling up to the hotel, she was directed to a valet, who offered to park her car. She chose to self-park. With the enthusiasm of a calf being led to slaughter, she approached the area on the front lawn where everyone had gathered to see the sunset, which unfortunately didn't live up to the hype. The sky was clear blue, but as often was the case with best laid plans, as soon as the sun neared the horizon, a rogue cloud mysteriously appeared, blocking the sun then dissipating, leaving a pallid smear of pinkish gray in it's wake. Then darkness. This was a far cry from the usually brilliant display of red and gold across the expansive sky. Everyone groaned, then the groans turned to laughter and chattering, as people turned to head into the hotel. The temperature had dropped ten degrees almost instantaneously.

Within seconds, the lawn was bare and everyone had gone inside to escape the cold. Marin looked up at the building as she climbed the front steps alone. The entranceway was certainly impressive, with the gold and glass railings and the courteous doormen dressed in regal-looking uniforms. She felt like a starlet in her calf-length slinky black dress, which sparkled under the lights. Her hair was pulled up into a pile on top of her head, her customary strands framing her face. She could feel the weight of her bold zirconia earrings. Her tension was slowly abating with the sound of Christmas music coming from somewhere.

Once inside the building, she marveled at the Christmas decorations. Immediately upon entering, Marin had caught sight of the life-size gingerbread house in the foyer. She had assisted with the newspaper article a week ago, describing these gingerbread houses in various hotels in Pima County and had been anxiously waiting to see this one. She walked through the assembled house, complete with Christmas decorations, and into the lounge on the other side, where she saw her workmates gathered. As she neared them, two girls from her department smiled at her and waved her over. She walked to them, smiling. A man with a tray offered her a glass of something sparkling. The girls were busy in conversation with someone she didn't know, so slowly, step-by-step, Marin inched away from them. They didn't notice.

Everyone else seemed so happy, while her guts were twisting into knots as she again started thinking about past events. Somehow, she didn't seem to fit in. Was it normal for her to feel alienated from everyone? Why couldn't she remember what she was like before? Marin was certain that she had been outgoing and lively. But then again, these people were basically strangers. She had left all her friends behind, for the second time in her life.

But there was more to it than just that. For her, as a crash survivor, this pain was compounded by grief for the loss of Tyler. She could now add to her losses an interesting man by the name of Adam. She hated facing the holidays. Guilt was rearing its ugly head. Why did I survive? Why not Tyler? It was days like this that she thought of that nice bubble bath.

Someone called her name and she turned around to see the two guys who worked in the typesetting department. She had heard that they were a couple, and this evening they made no attempt to hide the fact. They were standing alone, near a table, upon which stood an enormous poinsettia. Marin smiled and quickly walked over to join them. The three easily fell into conversation, which she welcomed with such relief. Jay and George were so real, so open, and they were making her laugh, which she sorely needed. She was suddenly glad that she had come to the party. These guys were pure magic, taking her to a whole new level of contentment and soundness.

George motioned them to a high table in the corner where the three took their drinks and their conversation. The table was situated by a railing and against floor to ceiling glass windows that covered the entire east side of the room. Two sets of glass doors were located off to one side, and were it not dark, the glass would reveal the expansive courtyard area outside. The courtyard, with its cushioned rattan furniture and atmospheric tiki torches, ended at a gently sloping set of stone stairs that led down to a massive pool, complete with loungers, colourful umbrellas and a poolside bar. Even during these winter months, tourists still flocked to Southern Arizona to bask in the warmish winter sunshine.

The men spoke of their jobs and about the party, occasionally pointing out people in the crowd that Marin didn't yet know.

"I'm sure you'll meet them soon enough," said Jay. "Especially Pam over there. She loves to talk about herself and her athleticism, particularly on the mountains, claiming to have once ran up the mountainside to Finger Rock."

With the mention of the mountains, Marin was able to turn the conversation to her experience in the Catalinas, on her hike from the pools. She was speaking about Adam and how she had unfortunately lost track of him.

"I just wish I could get in touch with him, to see how he's doing. He had a nasty fall, and although he played it cool, you could tell he was really rattled."

"But hey, you work for a newspaper!" said Jay enthusiastically.

Marin looked at him with a blank expression. "Meaning what?"

"You could contact the organizers of the El Tour and maybe get a list of participants. Or narrow it down to a list of Canadian participants. You are media! They love people like you; it's good advertising. Tell them you are writing a few follow-up stories on individual participants, where they come from, why they ride, that sort of thing. I don't know why they wouldn't indulge you, it's good exposure for them."

"I'd have to get permission from the editor to even pursue

the idea, wouldn't I? I mean, it would be something I wasn't assigned to."

George piped in, "Yes, but I really can't see them saying no. And they'll appreciate your enthusiasm in showing some initiative to get your own story in. You'd do your own research and interviewing. It would be good practice, and in the process, you just might weed out your mystery man."

Just then, they were summoned for dinner. As she turned to make her way to the ladies' room, she glanced up and saw Josh trying to get her attention. She hadn't seen him since she and Penelope were in Tubac. Turning back to George and Jay, Marin asked if she could sit with them. She felt comfortable in their presence, and wanted to avoid Josh at all cost. On the way to the dining room, the men waited for her as she made her restroom stop. Once seated at their table, Marin relaxed and smiled at her new friends. This was a good evening after all. She looked around for the waiter, feeling like she could use another glass of this bubbly stuff. The dining area was expansive, with green and gold carpet and glass partitions between sections of tables. The ceilings were high with wood-covered beams and pot lighting. A huge Christmas tree stood in the corner, covered in blue and gold bulbs and tinsel. The music had started, and the DJ was playing one of her favourite songs. "Come on, George," she said, grabbing the man's hand. "Let's dance!"

* * * *

THAT EVENING, AS SHE LAY alone in her bed, she was thinking of Tyler and the first time they made love. It had been here in

Arizona, beside the upper falls at Romero Pools, right after he asked her to marry him. They had been resting on a soft bed of grass, one of the rare green areas in their rocky surroundings. And it just happened. No hesitation, no debate. It wasn't uncomfortable or awkward, and it didn't require a lot of deliberation. It was easy and natural; they smiled the whole time, even laughed at one point. Afterwards, there was no "Did we make a mistake?" or "Should we not have?" or "I'm sorry we did . . ." It seemed as natural as eating or bathing or driving a car. She closed her eyes and cried. This was one small indulgence that she occasionally allowed herself.

16

THE EL TOUR DE TUCSON IS ONE OF THE LARGEST ROAD cycling events in the entire United States. The annual event, which features routes for riders of all levels, twists and weaves through and around the city of Tucson. This huge fundraising event is immensely popular to riders all over the continent. Cyclists enjoy this ride in particular, in part due to the climate and beauty of Tucson, as well as knowing their efforts raise millions of dollars annually to help the fight against cancer. The courses range from rolling to moderately hilly, as the city is surrounded by five mountain ranges. There is a great, fairly flat thirty-five-mile route, and that was the route that Marin and Tyler had ridden.

Marin felt a renewed optimism at the prospect of finding Adam. After little more than a brief conversation, her editor was not long in approving her request, which made her so happy, she giggled. She now felt she could prepare a convincing case to be asking for names of participants. Once all was in order, she was confident she was now ready to place the call. The first step was to make sure she was contacting the right person.

Putting on her best professional voice, Marin tried hard to sound cheerful and friendly yet determined.

"Hi, my name is Marin Jackson. I'm with the *Tucson Weekly*, and I'm looking for information about last November's ride. I'm doing an exposé on out-of-the-country riders. Just to talk to them about their experience, why they ride, etc. Firstly, I'm looking to do eastern Canada, perhaps starting with Toronto. Can you possibly give me some info on riders from that region?"

The response was cardboard. "We do that ourselves on our website. There's a link they go to, with a survey that covers their experiences and such."

Staying cheerful, Marin was not deterred. "Well, this would be of a more personal nature, about their experiences in Tucson, not only the ride. Something we would print in the paper. It would be still be good exposure for you as well. Also, I was hoping to speak with a few of them personally."

Mrs. Cardboard didn't budge. "Sorry, but I am not giving you any personal information about any of our riders."

"Well, I only need a few." Her spunk was beginning to wane. "Or maybe just one."

"It would be impossible, in this day and age, to contact any individual personally through us. There are many privacy rules in place, so we'd never give out that information. Can't you try social media? Put out a public request for participants."

Marin let out a big sigh, which she immediately realized would have been heard by the woman. She tried to sound cheerful again when she really wanted to yell at the woman. "Well, if I could give you some specific criteria, perhaps we could narrow down the search?"

"Well, it sounds like you want something really specific. What exactly are you searching for if not random participants?"

"Well, okay, the truth is, I'm actually only searching for one person." The sham was up. "A male rider, from Toronto. He would have been on the fifty-mile route, and I only know his first name."

"I understand. So, you are looking for a specific person. We can't do that."

"Please, I could really use your help." Marin realized that she had now resorted to grovelling. She felt pathetic.

Hearing Marin's words, the woman's voice softened. "Well, I'm telling you I can't do that. But let me think. Here's what I can maybe do. If you'd like, I could possibly send a message to this person and ask him if he wanted to be 'found' by you, so if you just give me his name and yours, I'll see what I can do."

"No, you don't quite understand. As I've mentioned, I don't exactly know his name. Well, I only know his first name, that he's from Toronto, and that he rode in the fifty-mile division. Surely you have a database whereby you could filter either by first name or by category or age group, or by home city?"

"Yes, but I can't give that to you. Are you chasing someone with whom you had a moment?"

"Well, it was an encounter, but not in the way you might think. Would you be willing to do the search for me and find him, and then contact him and ask him if he wanted to contact me?" Marin paused. "Can you do that for me?" She suddenly realized how stupid this must sound to the woman on the other end of the line.

"I'm sorry, and who did you say you were? Did you say you're from the paper?"

Marin sat further back in her chair. This was going to take longer than she thought. She would need to use another approach. "Okay, here it is. I am with the paper, but why I am calling is personal. I met this man, his name is Adam, on the day after the ride. It was in the Catalina Mountains, and he was hurt, right at the top, near Romero Pools. I helped him down and an ambulance took him to the hospital, and I visited him the next day. Now, he's gone and I didn't have the chance to see him again. I just want to make sure he's okay, to say I'm sorry I didn't make it to see him again. I was working and I showed up late, and it was too late and he was gone. And I don't know if he's okay, after the fall and all." Marin was blathering.

Now, it was the woman's turn to sigh. "So, why didn't you just say so?"

"I thought it sounded lame and unimportant, and I had a feeling it wouldn't be something I could just ask for," Marin responded, considerably quieter this time.

"And you were right. It's not. As I've said, there are privacy issues in play here and I can't give you any information." Her voice became hushed. "But I will look into it. I will check the database, but if you tell anyone that I'm doing this, it would be very bad for me, so please don't. So, if you just give me your information, in detail, all I can promise is that *if* I do find him, I will send a message to him with your information. You won't ever hear from me because I don't know you, right?"

"Yes! Right! Thank you," gushed Marin. "I don't know you, and you don't know me. I can do that."

After the woman had taken Marin's contact information, she said, "I have no idea how long this will take, or if it will happen, so you'll need to go about your days and just wait. Remember, you won't hear from me. And if you don't hear from him, it's because either I couldn't find him, or he didn't want to contact you. I will not pressure this person; I will only send him a note. It's the best I can offer you."

"I am very grateful that you are even trying, so yes, I do understand."

The woman said goodbye, and Marin sat back, a smile on her face. This, at least, was something.

17

Adam sat back and looked at the calendar on his desk. He had been waiting for Steve's call for a while. It felt like a very long time, and he couldn't quite remember what day it was that they had spoken. He had only been in the office long enough to pour himself a cup of coffee. Anya had not yet arrived. This was one of those lovely rare moments when the office was still. All he could hear was the faint sound of music from the audio system. So, when his phone rang and the call display said "Steve Henderson," he grabbed the phone, almost dropping it in his haste.

"Hello, is this Steve?" Adam exhaled and spoke in a calm and even voice, trying not to be overly optimistic. He stood and walked across his office to shut the door. Anya had just walked in the office and this conversation was not for public consumption.

"Buffalo."

"Excuse me?" asked Adam.

"Dad's name is Keith Murphy and he moved to Buffalo with his wife about two years ago, or a bit more. The word is he was not a very popular man, had a few shady business dealings. And he wasn't easy to find. Apparently, their move was very sudden, and it's hard to say why. Keith had some unsavoury friends who used to gather at this farmhouse outside of town. Somebody died there, but the case went nowhere because everyone present told the same story—exactly the same story, like they had rehearsed it. I'm discovering tidbits about a Mexican man as well, who was once in the area but seemed to leave not long after the Murphys. Anyway, Keith dissolved his company, left everything to his foreman to deal with, and left. Parts of the story are still unclear. Some months later, a realtor was contacted by a numbered company to put their house on the market."

"Any news about Tyler?" Adam asked, not being able to hide his anxiousness.

"Yeah, the kid. He was banged up pretty bad. He was in a coma for quite some time, plus he lost a leg. Actually, he was still in a coma when the family moved him to a head trauma center in Chicago. I can see moving him there, but did the entire family need to pull up roots and leave? It seems odd to me. Wow, looking at the medical report if that kid lived, he'd need a lot of therapy. My neighbour's kid had a similar accident. Had head damage and lost a leg, and he was messed up for a long time. He's never been quite right, and I think he's still in group therapy.

But this is where it gets interesting. There's no record of Tyler beyond that. There's no death certificate in Washington, nor in Illinois. The funny thing is, although I tracked them to Illinois there's no record of them actually living there. And if they lived somewhere else before they moved to New York, I haven't found anything to that effect. I tried searching national death records and still came up empty. I haven't found a coroner's report anywhere. Having said that, I haven't found any proof of life, either. So, it's hard to say what happened to him."

"So maybe something is wrong with the story, like Marin suspected," said Adam, more a statement than a question.

"It makes you wonder, that's for sure. So, getting back to Tyler's family. His mom's name is Barbara. It looks like Mr. Murphy may have resumed business in the Buffalo region under his wife's maiden name. And I am still looking in to the Mexican guy. I heard something about a cartel, so I'm checking that out as well. Okay, that's that. Now, hang on a minute. I have to put the phone down."

Adam could hear papers shuffling around. He then realized he hadn't been writing anything down. Steve came back to the phone.

"Sorry about that," he said. "Okay, as for the young lady Marin, her name is Marin Jackson. She was listed in the police report as the other body at the site of the crash. She was the driver of the vehicle. She's in Arizona now, and her father and younger sister still live in the Kirkland area of Washington. Dad is Geoffrey Jackson, a local plumber. Sister, Lauren, is in her senior year at Kirkland Secondary. Mother, Angie, deceased. She apparently died under somewhat suspicious circumstances. Her car was found at a pullout along Chuckanut Drive, the engine running. Her body was found down below. An autopsy revealed a lot of alcohol in her system, and her neck was broken. There didn't appear to be any foul play, but still at the time, the death was ruled as suspicious. Dad had an alibi, and the Murphys had already moved away. I have no idea if the case is still active. The last report I saw said it could still possibly have been a suicide. Oh—and she had been seen with the Mexican."

"So that's it then," said Adam after a pause. "Well, I don't know how to thank you, Steve. This is a lot of information, and I'm not quite sure what to do with it. You found out a lot of stuff here! Buffalo, eh?" Adam was wondering if he wasn't a bit out of his league here. "Oh, and am I required to pay you? I'm sorry, but we haven't discussed money. Can you please send me a bill?"

"Nah, we're sorta related. This one's on me, Doc. I'm happy to help," said the big voice, with a deep laugh. "I'm still poking around, because it seems this is all related to an ongoing case here, so I might be able to find something to hand over to local authorities. Such as, Keith Murphy's whereabouts." Just before hanging up, he added, "And good luck, I hope you find what you are looking for."

Unsure what to do next, Adam grabbed a pad of paper and a pen. He wanted to write some of this stuff down before he forgot. *What are the names again? Keith Murphy, Tyler Murphy, Marin Jackson. Oh—and Barbara Murphy. What is the name of Marin's father?* He thought Geoffrey. *Yes, it's Geoffrey.* Grabbing hold of his tepid coffee, Adam leaned back in his chair. It was great to have this information, although he still didn't know what to do with it.

Standing, Adam went over to reopen his office door. He had to make it evident that he was accessible. Sitting down again, he opened his computer and typed "Keith Murphy Buffalo." He got nothing. He tried "Barbara Murphy Buffalo," then "Tyler." Still nothing. He did a map search of Buffalo to see how far away it was. He had never been there but was grateful that it was less than a two-hour drive away. It could have been worse; it could have been Texas or Oklahoma. Still, his searches had all come up empty. Slamming the lid of his computer in frustration, he went out to the waiting room to see Anya. She would have ready his schedule for the day. A trip to Buffalo was prominently on the back of his mind.

18

That evening, Adam again dialled Steve Henderson's number. "Steve, I'm going to give you my email address. I was busy trying to absorb our conversation when we last spoke, and I wonder if you could send me some more detail. For example, do you have an address for the Murphys in Buffalo? I don't think you gave it to me. I was too busy focusing on names. I've tried every search possible, and of course, they would be unlisted, so I've had no luck finding them. Much obliged, Steve." He left his email address and hung up the phone. This was tricky business, made more problematic by the fact that he had no idea what he was doing. But he felt his blood pressure rise as he realized he was enjoying this enigma, the curiosity of this peculiar situation.

Checking his messages the next morning, he was happy to see that Steve did send the message. He'd call later to thank the man. The following weekend, having no plans, Adam decided to drive to Buffalo to see where the Murphys lived. It was a clear and windy day. His GPS was set and it looked like it would take him just under two hours to get there. The address was apparently in a neighbourhood known as Allentown. He had no idea what he would do when he got there, thinking an idea might come to him by the time he arrived. He was not oblivious to the fact that it was a stupid thing to think.

Adam made good time, and once over the border, he easily made his way to the Allentown district. He found it to be a very old but artsy district, lots of Victorian style homes, many cafés and restaurants, and many large wall murals. He imagined it looked better in the summer, green and more alive. Everything looked bleak and dead in the winter. There was a very obvious difference between cities and towns in the United States than in Canada, although he never could quite put his finger on it. One building of particular note was a stunning mansion on Delaware Street. Adam slowed down to examine the impressive architecture of this well-preserved building, which he noticed was now a boutique hotel.

He explored the streets for a few minutes longer before allowing his GPS to take him to the address. He finally arrived at the block, a heavily treed section of West Avenue. The houses were unimpressive, and when he pulled up to the Murphy house, he saw before him a tired-looking and unkempt two-story brick-and-vinyl-siding house. The street was void of activity. Actually, it seemed like nobody was alive, as there was not a soul in sight. Not a single vehicle drove by. Parking a few doors down, he sat in his car with the engine running. It was too cold to switch off. "Now what?" he said to himself. He thought of asking a neighbour about the family, but what would he ask? He didn't want to draw attention to himself. He had Canadian plates, and he might look like a stalker or something, just sitting there. He decided to drive to a coffee shop to grab a sandwich and think. Maybe Claire was right—maybe he wasn't cut out for this.

Adam pulled out onto the road and turned right a few times until he came to what appeared to be a main shopping street. Driving slowly, he spotted a delicatessen across the street, so he parked his car and ran across the road. The little bell on the door rang as he entered the building. He was instantly aware of the smell of processed meat and potato salad. He grabbed a small table along the wall before he realized this was self-serve. There was a man and a woman behind the counter. The man was serving a line of customers at the deli while the woman was serving those wanting coffee and lunch items. He figured it was likely a husband-and-wife business. He went to the latter line and ordered himself a coffee and a large bowl of soup. He was given a number to take to his table, where he retreated with his coffee.

Sitting down, he took in his surroundings. This was a quaint little place, with old wooden windows, red plaid curtains, and a big sign over the door that read *"God Bless America."* The radio was playing familiar sounding country music, although he didn't know the artist. As he sat there, he was running over different scenarios as a form of introduction if he were to knock on the door: *"Hello, Mr. Murphy? You don't know me from Adam,"* he added a bit of humour there, *"but I'd like to know if your son is alive or dead." Or how about, "Hi there, Mr. Murphy, could I please see your son's death certificate?"* The very pleasant girl arrived with his soup, and he ate it hungrily, feeling somewhat nervous and a little uneasy. Luckily, nobody could tell what he was up to.

Suddenly, as if by miracle, a woman walked into the store and headed to the deli case. She was a nondescript woman, a bit dishevelled, and Adam didn't really pay her any attention until he heard the deli guy call out, "Hello, Mrs. Murphy, how are you?" His voice boomed over the counter.

Did he just say Mrs. Murphy? How likely is it that this is the same Murphy? Adam froze, his spoon midway to his mouth. He lowered it slowly, waiting for the woman to answer. She was soft spoken and he had a hard time detecting what was being said. One thing he knew for certain, and that was that she wanted ham.

Adam, thinking he'd better move fast, jumped up and strode to the counter to pay his bill. The woman walked past him and headed for the door. Without waiting for the girl to ring in his meal, he left a ten-dollar bill on the counter. He wanted to get out of there in a hurry. Much too large a tip, but Adam didn't want to let the woman slip away from him. If anyone were to notice what he was about to do, he'd be in big trouble. He planned on following her.

She turned right, which indicated the possibility that she was heading to the Murphy house. He grabbed his fob and unlocked his car door. Then when he realized she was on foot, he hit the fob again and relocked the door. He didn't want to get too close, so he slowed down, looking around as he tried hard to lag and appear nonchalant. If she were to go in a different direction he would turn around and leave. But she didn't. She turned right again and headed down West Avenue. As they approached the house, she did cross the street, then the lawn, and she headed for the front door. Unsure what to do, Adam hesitated before continuing on the opposite side of the street. Attempting to appear as if he had a destination, he looked straight ahead and walked faster in order to pass the house, since he couldn't just turn around and start walking back from where he came. But as the woman opened the door, she turned around and looked him straight in the eye. He looked away, but not before she locked her eyes on him and held the stare until he passed. He felt stupid pretending not to notice her. Only then did she disappear inside, slamming the door. She knew.

Adam kept walking and turned right at the next corner. He picked up his pace to almost a run as he again turned right at the next intersection. Ahead, he could see the deli and his car. He hurriedly crossed the street and unlocked the car doors as he approached his vehicle. As he reached for the door handle, he noticed a movement out of the corner of his eye. The red-checkered curtain in the deli was moving. He was certain that someone was watching him. He got into his car and quickly glanced over. It looked like the man who had served Mrs. Murphy. Starting the engine, Adam put the car into gear and headed for the highway. This place gave him the creeps.

19

HAVING CALLED CLAIRE A FEW TIMES, ADAM DISCOVERED that she had been out on photo shoots for most of the week, but he did manage to catch up with her. It was a snowy Tuesday, and he had arranged to leave work early, to get ahead of the weather. He then texted ahead to be sure that she would be at home. Adam pulled into the drive and collected his thoughts, unsure of the reception he would get when posing his questions to her.

Adam braced the wind as he locked his car. Walking to the front door, he kicked the snow from his boots before entering. His dad, Ben, who happened to be walking into the kitchen at that moment, greeted Adam as he was taking off his coat.

"Hi, Adam, what are you doing out on a day like today? The roads must be bad. You look cold. Can I get you a drink?"

"No, thanks, Dad. I just came to talk to Claire," Adam responded, as he walked into the kitchen to catch up with his dad. "Is she in her darkroom?"

Ben nodded. "I haven't figured out if she goes in there to get away from me, or if she gets off on the fumes," he said with a laugh.

"Maybe a bit of both. After all, it is her meditation room. Perhaps she goes in for a nap," offered Adam. "I'll take that drink then, Dad, if I have to wait for her to finish up."

It was true that Claire loved her darkroom. With digital photography, Claire's job was much easier, but she would still use her darkroom for special shots. She had once defended her preferences, saying to Ben, "Did you know it can take up to three bracketed RAW digital files to achieve the same sort of tonal range some films can get?" He had no idea what she meant, but he made certain to agree with her.

Just as his dad reached for the cups, Claire emerged, drying her hands on a towel. Cheerfully, she insisted on making lattes for everyone and immediately busied herself.

Adam sat at one of the stools at the island and began, "Well, I still don't know if Tyler is dead or alive. I found the parents, but there were no clues as to the son."

Claire stopped what she was doing and asked, "What do you mean, you found the parents?"

Adam explained what had taken place on his trip to Buffalo. When Adam had described his experience with Mrs. Murphy, Ben added sarcastically, "Well, I'm surprised you didn't pitch a tent in front of their house and wait for movement."

Ignoring his dad, Adam's gaze shifted to Claire. She wore the same expression as Ben. Ignoring that, he asked her, "What about Phil? Doesn't he work for Interpol or something?"

Phil was Kate's boyfriend, who had provided some assistance to the investigation around the death of Will and the vehicular assault on Claire. But that had been years ago, and Adam didn't know Phil at all. He only had a few brief social encounters with him over the years, when Adam was still a boy.

"Oh, Adam, I think he's retired now. Besides, they only look for criminals and terrorists. You know, people who impose real threats to the nation. I don't know if you could make a strong enough case on why Interpol should help you look for this guy. Phil has been retired for about eight years. He grows vegetables now."

"Yes, but he must still have friends in the business?" Adam said, still pressing Claire.

She responded by saying, "Adam, look at what just happened in Paris, with the mass shootings at the Bataclan concert hall. I think Interpol is likely still very busy with that, and I'm sure it would take priority. Did Nigel help you? I thought he put you in touch with Joe's cousin?" She handed Adam a latte.

"He did, and it was great, but I could use his help again. I just don't know if I should keep calling him. I feel like I'm taking advantage."

Claire let out a big sigh. "I don't know what to say. If this is something you really want to pursue, it sounds like this man is your best bet. I guess you'll need to go back with your hat in your hand," she said, as she handed the second latte to Ben.

Adam agreed with Claire. She was right. He'd call the man again and explain he wasn't prepared for their last conversation. He had not taken notes; he didn't recall the name of the company that Mr. Murphy had started up, in his wife's maiden name. Could he please provide that again? Although truthfully, Adam didn't know if that new information would help him. Surely there must be an easy way to find out if someone was alive or dead! But for the time being, he had to call Steve again.

"Or you could just pay the man and stop asking for favours," came back Ben.

"Thanks, Dad, and you are right saying I should pay him, especially if I will need him again." Adam sighed, running his hand across his chin, realizing he was in need of a shave. With his questions being answered, he finished his coffee quickly.

After saying goodbye, Adam stepped outside to face the elements. He still had a few errands to run before returning home but decided first to return to his office, as it was on his way. He would call Steve from there, this time with pen and paper in hand.

Adam reached the man easily this time. Steve, friendly and accommodating as usual, began telling Adam that he had searched the SSDI, using the previous address, Social Security number and date of birth, which fortunately he had, courtesy of the Portland soccer club, the police accident report, and Tyler's school records. He had obtained all possible information, even using both addresses in Washington and New York, and he came up with nothing. So, he firmly believed "the guy" was still alive.

"We are also trying to find out more about the other man. The Mexican. Apparently, he's a wanted man, so he remains a person of interest in connection with both families."

Adam felt a sense of anticipation. "So, Marin could be right about Tyler. But then, where the hell is he? This might be crazy, but I was thinking that Tyler could possibly work for his dad? I don't know why I thought of that, but if he's alive, he must be doing something. Unless he's in a home for invalids somewhere. Who knows how badly he was hurt? I'm sorry, but I didn't write anything down last time we spoke. I wasn't very prepared. Can you please give me that business information again? Either now, or you can email it to me?"

"I'm sure I have that written down somewhere. I'll check my notes and get you the company information and anything else I've found. You could be right, possibly the son works for him and would be on the employee directory. And how about the girl's family? Want me to look for anything there?"

Adam was thrilled. "Actually, yes, I'd appreciate it if you did that!"

The man was deadpan as he spoke. "I was being sarcastic."

Adam was speechless. He would need to carefully formulate his next response. The last thing he wanted to do was piss this guy off. "I'm sorry, Steve, I really am. I'm not thinking straight. You have done more than enough for me already."

Steve replied, "Let me put it this way, this is your last chance to ask me anything. I think we need to agree to have an end date to this. At some point, you have to realize the only way to find out if he's alive is to go knock on the friggin' door and just ask them. Why don't you just do that?"

"I know you're right, but even you said that this Keith guy was a shady character. Maybe he did have something to do with the death of Marin's mom? I don't know why they would have been so careful to hide themselves. I'm guessing they wouldn't appreciate a stranger snooping around. I remember Marin was afraid of Keith and she thought he was capable of things. I guess I shouldn't take that literally, eh? But given his questionable past, I'm trying different ways. For now, anyway. Besides, I still don't know if Tyler wants to be found. Maybe he does hold Marin responsible for the accident. I need to know what can of worms I might be opening here."

Steve answered calmly, "I'm sure this is hard for you, and I must admit, I love a good mystery as much as anyone. I guess it's why being a cop like my dad wasn't exciting enough. So, okay, I'll check that out about the new company. I might as well check out the girl while I'm at it, so you won't be calling me again in a weeks' time."

Adam said thank you, but then added, "Steve, to make this fair to both of us, I think down the road I need to pay you for any extra work. I may call you again, depending on what I find out. I don't know how else I would do this between Toronto and Seattle, and I might really need you. Would that work for you?"

"Let me do this, and we'll talk about it going forward. It might not be worth your while."

Adam had heard this man was a machine when it came to his job. There wasn't much he couldn't find out. Adam would need to thank both Nigel and Joe. Within the hour, Adam was leaving his office again, still having a few stops to make on his way home. To save time, he decided to take a different route. As he was passing through a quiet neighbourhood as a short-cut, he entered an intersection where he noticed a large sign in front of the church on the corner. It read, *"Wednesdays 7 p.m. Group Therapy; Thursday 8 p.m. Grief Counselling Workshop"*

Of course! What was it that Steve had said? *"My neighbour's kid was messed up for a long time and is still in group therapy."* Why didn't he think of it sooner? But that was just another challenge. He doubted there was a master directory of group therapy sessions for adult males with head injuries in Buffalo. Another thing prominent on Adam's mind was the fact that he had no idea where Marin was. He would need to find her eventually if he was to connect these two. The one thing he did remember was that Marin was planning on going to Romero Pools on Tyler's birthday, which was in April. He still had time to make this work.

20

Marin had recovered from the stress of the holidays. The weeks now flew by as she immersed herself in her work. When she wasn't working, she was enjoying life as best she could, although, at times, she felt a little like Linus because of the perpetual cloud she felt over her head.

Every Sunday, she would hike with her group. They stayed away from the Catalinas and Sabino Canyon because of the cold and snow at higher elevations, but Marin was more than happy with Pima Canyon and hikes like the Wild Burro Trail on Dove Mountain, never tiring of the beauty of the canyon walls and the towering jagged rock formations. It wouldn't be long before the spring colours would erupt in the desert, with flora often waking up by early to mid February. The colours were always awe-inspiring, with everything from California Poppies and Lupines to blooming saguaros and prickly pear. Her personal favourites were the delicate fairy dusters and the brilliant magenta cholla.

Saturdays, she would be on the Loop trails with Penelope, having finally coaxed her friend to get out on her bike. Marin herself had not ridden in years, since before her accident, but was willing to give it a try. She was very optimistic but quickly discovered that her balance was not what it used to be. Penelope was wobbling alongside her, and they did manage a few short rides with no mishaps, inching their way while occasionally running into each other. Aside from a few random strange looks from passersby, they returned unscathed. This brought with it another feeling of success, another hurdle overcome, and each outing was better than the previous.

What brought Marin the greatest comfort was spending time with her new friends, Jay and George. Since their introduction at the company Christmas party, they had begun spending more and more time together. The three had quickly become the best of friends during that evening's dinner. Now George would drag Marin out to every art festival or concert they attended, and Jay was forever introducing her to a new restaurant. The two of them were real foodies and would often take her long distances just to watch her eat their favourite foods. Over a drink, Jay would share all of the gossip at the newspaper and give her little tips on how to deal with certain people in the newsroom, while George rolled his eyes. He believed in minding ones own business.

Today, they were taking her to the Mission San Xavier del Bac. Marin had often seen it on drives to Green Valley or Tubac—a ghostly elegant white edifice, Moorish-looking and mysterious, perched on a small hill a short distance from the highway. George, being of Mexican heritage, said he comes every year to honour his maternal grandfather, who, at one time, would come to the mission annually on a pilgrimage. His grandfather, later moving to the area, had then devoted his last years working on the restoration of the crumbling building.

"The Mission was established some time in the late 1600s

by an Italian Jesuit," George was explaining to her from the back seat. Jay and George would take turns driving, with Marin always riding in the front passenger seat. "They have church services every Sunday, and the nuns who work there still live in the Mission convent." Jay pulled into the gravel parking lot and they got out of the car. Marin marvelled at the sight of the mission up close, having watched it grow bigger and bigger as the car neared the building.

As they walked the exterior grounds, Marin found herself overwhelmed with the beauty of this old historic building. She had never felt so small as she did now in its presence, not even when climbing in the mountains. It was not because of the size but rather what it represented. The delicate detail of the impressive architecture in the entranceway contrasted sharply against the primitive medieval wood doors. The east tower was missing the dome on top, but George explained it was still under restoration.

"Before we go inside, let's take a walk up Martinez Hill. We'll show you the lion monuments as well as the shrine. I think you'll like them. Then we'll check out the view at the top." George appeared impassioned as he spoke.

Marin felt an unfamiliar serenity. She had felt calm, but not like this. They had been climbing in silence when she finally asked them, "How did you two meet? You are incredibly well suited. It's like you guys were born a couple."

They both laughed, and it was Jay who answered first.

"We met when we were eighteen, at high school gradua-tion. I went to a different school, but that year Pima County held a huge outdoor graduation event that involved three districts. It was some kind of anniversary for the district's . . . I don't know what. But we met there."

George cut in saying, "We just knew. We saw each other and started talking, and it was like we both knew we'd be together forever. For me, there was no secret to the success. It just happened"

Jay was nodding. "I couldn't imagine being anywhere else. Believe me, we have differences. But doesn't everyone? It's no big deal to either of us. After all, we are two unique individuals and we don't try to sway each other. We live independently but together, does that make sense?"

George surprised Marin by saying, "And obviously we've grown together, into each others' habits and ways. But we've been together for over twenty years now, and it doesn't feel any different."

"Twenty years! How can that be? Were you ten when you met?" Marin responded, a surprised look on her face.

George laughed. "Marin, we are both forty-one."

Marin smiled up at them. They were now at the top of the hill, enjoying the view of the Mission below. Jay was smiling back. She had never seen teeth so white. Jay was tall, strong looking. He was very handsome; he could easily have been a model. His sandy brown hair was worn short and he had one of those perpetual facial stubbles that Marin could never quite understand. George, in contrast, was very dark, accounting for his Spanish heritage. His wavy hair was pulled back tightly in a man-bun. While standing nearly as tall, his frame was slight.

"I get it. It's exactly how Tyler and I were, although we lost the chance to be together for a very long time. But we could never make people understand the ease of our relationship. They kept saying we were too young to know for sure. But we knew! Whenever I looked at him, I saw myself."

They turned around to head back down the hill. Jay let out a big sigh. "It's like people keep waiting for us to fail. We don't know if this will last forever; nobody ever does know. But that's not the point. It's real now and that's what matters."

George added, "Someone once told me that I was with Jay out of laziness. That I took the easy way out and just settled for the first person who came along, and I might be missing out on a whole bunch of fabulous partners."

Jay looked at him in horror. "Who said that?" to which George replied, "I'm not telling." He turned to wink at Marin.

Once they returned to the Mission, Jay took her by the hand. "Now, we'll go inside."

Marin gasped at the sight of the interior. It was hard not to be awestruck by the main altar in the chapel, dazzling with gold and red against a blue background. She slowly walked around viewing the frescoes, Jay and George allowing her all the time she wanted. After Marin had taken it all in, George led her back to the wooden statue of St. Francis, who lay under a blanket, behind a partition of glass. George turned to Marin and said, "Do you know what *milagro* means?"

Marin shook her head, "No, I don't."

"It means miracle. People come here to pray for a miracle, and the story is that many of those miracles have been granted."

"But I don't pray," said Marin, almost apologetically. "I've never been to church and I don't know how to pray."

George smiled and placed his hand on her shoulder. "There are many ways of praying. I'm sure you pray in your own way when you are lost in those thoughts of yours. I'm sure you have asked for miracles, too, haven't you?"

Jay added, "I've learned that there are really no rules for doing this, Marin. Sometimes, people leave pieces of jewellery or even a pillow or a blanket. Or we can take you to the gift shop where you can buy a little metal charm, and you can use that. Other people just leave handwritten notes. Here, we've brought you some paper. Let's go over there so you can write a note."

Marin felt tears coming to her eyes. These two had brought her all this way so that she could ask St. Francis for a miracle— to bring Tyler back to her. She could hardly see through her tears as she tried to write down the words.

21

Marin sat in the car, her forehead pressed against the glass as she watched the mission disappear from sight. As George's car neared the freeway exit, Marin looked at them and said, "I'm not ready to go home yet. It's only three o'clock. Are you guys hungry? We could stop at that little Italian place on Skyline?"

Her friends answered yes in unison, and so George, who was now driving, turned right at the light and headed along Speedway towards Campbell. The radio was playing the Moody Blues. Of all songs, it was "I Know You're Out There Somewhere." Marin turned up the volume and, putting her head back, closed her eyes. Her thoughts turned to Adam as she remembered that his mom had picked songs for him at times of need. Maybe, if his mom was here, she might have picked this song now, for Marin. She felt George's hand pat her knee gently.

While not close to her home, the Catalina Foothills neighbourhood was only a short twenty-minute drive from where she lived. This was quite an upscale place to live, but she loved browsing through the shops and the restaurants at La Encantada, the open-air shopping center. At this intersection, there was something fabulous on all four corners, her favourite being this one where they now found themselves. George parked the car, and the three of them slowly ambled up the staircase to the restaurant. Marin looked at her companions and humorously commented on how windblown and tired they all looked.

"You can't possibly be tired, a young thing your age," teased Jay.

The host seated them at the long bar table and took their drink orders. Marin asked for a Corona, to which Jay put up his hand in protest. "Don't drink that cat piss, Marin. Let me order you a nice beer." He looked at the waiter and said, "Please bring us a couple of Kilt Lifters."

"A couple of what?" said Marin, a look of disbelief on her face.

"Trust me, you'll love it. Don't let the name fool you. It's from a local brewery up in Tempe. We'll take you there some day."

The waiter came back with the rich, amber-coloured ale, which Marin agreed tasted wonderful. The waiter dropped some menus on the table, and for a while they were left to their drinks and conversation. Once they had ordered their food, Jay turned to her and said, "Marin, there's something I've always wanted to ask you: What was it like being in a coma?"

Marin looked stunned for a moment. She looked at him and her jaw dropped open. Her mouth moved but no words came out.

"Oh God, I'm so sorry," he fumbled. "I shouldn't have asked you."

"No, it's fine. It just caught me off guard, but it's okay.

I guess I would say that I didn't really feel anything until I started to wake up all those months later. They moved my room when I started to stir, apparently. But I didn't really wake up for another few weeks. During that time, I would hear the odd word, far away, like in a dream. Some of it was scary, like a bad dream. I could sense when someone was near me, but that's about it. But the whole time before that, I felt absolutely nothing. I was shocked when they told me how long I was in there."

"Did you feel different afterwards?" asked George.

"Well, I fidget more," she said, as she refolded her napkin for the fifth time. "And I think I laugh less. You know what I mean. Really laugh, like I do when I'm with you two. You guys are magic for me. You make me feel weightless. But for a very long time, I didn't laugh. I still have problems with my long-term memory, and I think I'm a bit more forgetful. But I can't remember," Marin said jocosely, winking at George. "And I seem to think that I used to be more outgoing. Another weird thing is that I still confuse reality with dreams. My doctor says that feeling will slowly go away."

"It must have been a terrible accident."

Marin sat in thought before she answered, "Yes, it must have been. I'm glad I don't remember it. Dad wouldn't let me see the car." Marin pushed the napkin away and placed her hands in her lap, determined not to fidget. "You know, I've been starting to think I didn't overhear my dad talking about Tyler. Maybe that was just a dream or a hallucination? Maybe it was because I wanted so badly for it to be true."

Then trying to change the subject, she said, "Hey, guys, I can't thank you enough for today. This has been wonderful."

The atmosphere was vibrant, the music loud. People were coming and going; there were tables full of patrons laughing loudly and toasting to just about anything. Young women were arriving in packs, ready to party, while the waiters bustled about attentively. The concept was open-kitchen, and from where Marin sat, she could watch the waiters slice into the huge loaves of bread and baguettes, freshly baked and piled along the countertop. The smells coming from the kitchen were rife with herbs and garlic.

George leaned over to Marin to be heard above the din. "What about your Romero Pools guy? Did the lady from El Tour get back to you?"

"She asked me not to call her; said she'd call me."

"But that was nearly two months ago! Do you think she forgot?"

Marin had again started fidgeting with her napkin. "I couldn't say. But you know, I think it's likely too late. It would have been nice to know he was okay and to say goodbye. But it didn't happen. I'm sure he's forgotten all about me by now, so to contact him after all this time might just be weird." Even as she spoke the words, she knew she would be calling the woman again to see if she had made any progress.

On the drive home, Marin was thinking of her living situation. She was grateful that Stella spent time away, and it was likely for this reason that the woman had advertised for a roommate. Yet, there were times Marin wished she was going home to a place she could call her own, with her own furnishings in styles of her choosing, her little Talavera pots on the shelf. She hoped that soon she could afford that, but in the mean time, she was again grateful that Stella was away. As the car pulled up to the door, Marin picked up her bag and got out of the car. Both Jay and George got out to hug her.

"Thanks guys, that was just the best day and I had a wonderful time," she said. Walking into the house, she thought to herself that today had indeed been a good day, and her good days were very important.

22

ADAM HAD SPENT THE DAY IN TORONTO, AT A CONFERENCE of Psychotherapy professionals. He was aware that he wasn't fully engaged with the lecture that was currently underway. It had been a long day, and he was becoming restless. Adam had come looking for answers, which he didn't get. Afterwards five or six of his colleagues had plans to go for a meal and a drink at The Brewhouse, which was situated on the waterfront. Adam was invited and agreed to go along.

After a round of drinks had been delivered, Adam decided to dive right in with his question, which he delivered to no one in particular. "If I had a client with a unique situation, would it help if he could meet someone in a similar circumstance to whom he could relate? I would try to connect the two through a practitioner who had identified one of their patients as having a similar set of circumstances. How likely would it be to make that happen? What if I needed to find a better way to relate to him. Would that be possible, to look for a peer situation?"

"I don't know how plausible it would be. How could you demonstrate the validity or the necessity of such a thing?" answered one woman seated directly across from him. She had a concerned look on her face.

"And how would you go about it?" asked another.

"I could put a notice out to practitioners in the area, looking for patients with specific issues. The result being that this could possibly help one of their patients as well. I know that suitable referrals are what make group sessions work, and that the dropout rate can be high. The odds could be good to find a match that would work for both sides."

"So, this would be used as a frame of reference for you, is that it?" was another skeptical comment.

"This might be what is termed as a non-legitimate referral, more to assist with training and to find a match for my client. There are specific concerns I have, and I thought it would make him feel more comfortable hearing someone with similar issues speak. I found some valuable reading and useful suggestions from Roller (1977) and Spitz (1976) on building collaborative relationships, and it gave me the idea to try this.

My client suffers from anxiety and only partially listens, as he feels he can't relate to anyone. I'm afraid I might lose him, and I'm afraid he might harm himself." Adam wasn't completely comfortable with this charade, although having this information might actually help someone.

"Well, how would you go about it if, say, you did come up with someone?"

"I'm hoping I could sit in on a few sessions in the beginning to determine the suitability. I'm looking for universality and altruism so my patient can develop some self-understanding. I thought maybe I could reach out to some doctors in, say, Buffalo."

"But why Buffalo, if I might ask? They will wonder why you are not doing this in Toronto." It was the woman across the table again.

"I considered it might be safer for all involved, as looking locally would be less anonymous. Privacy issues and all, the client would have a better likelihood of remaining unidentified. Or I could say I haven't been able to find any suitable parallels here?"

There were shakes of the heads and nods, and much murmuring, but nobody could really agree one way or the other. At the end, the general consensus was that the APA had stringent confidentiality rules and there were no databases, so this might not be as easy as it sounds.

Adam sat back in his chair and said, "It was a long shot anyway. But please, if any of you happen to know of a physiotherapist in the Buffalo area who would be willing to speak with me, I'd appreciate it. Even if it was just for them to tell me it was an impossibility."

A round of nods followed, and the topic ended. Adam sat in silence, listening to his colleagues discuss things like weather, kids, and work. He sensed none of them would follow up. He was feeling discouraged but hadn't given up yet.

Adam's efforts to find new ways to locate Tyler were finally giving him some more unconventional ideas. His next plan involved calling his friend, although he did feel some hesitancy about involving him. But the following evening, he called Pete and asked if he had time for lunch. He had a favour to ask him.

"Let me come out your way," was Pete's response. "I have to be in the city next Sunday, if that will work for you."

The following Sunday, they met in a noisy bar in Mississauga, just minutes from the freeway. It didn't take long for Adam to get right to it. "How'd you like to come with me to Buffalo?"

"Why did I think this might happen?" said Pete, his head collapsing onto the table, his hands covering his ears.

"I don't really know what I'm doing. I'm trying to find out if Tyler is in therapy, in a facility, or if he's even in Buffalo. I'm just pulling at straws here. What I want is to know if he's alive and I'm looking for a subtle way to do it. So, I was thinking, what if I was to put out a flyer looking for people willing to take part in a study of trauma victims or something like that? And we could randomly drop one on their doorstep?"

"I dunno, man. I mean, is this even ethical?"

"Why does everyone say that? I think it is, because I really am interested in speaking with him as a trauma victim and also to help him get to Marin, if that's what he wants."

"What if he doesn't? What if he's got amnesia or something and he doesn't even know who she is? Maybe he never liked her and was glad to get away from her? Or maybe he doesn't live here, but he's in a facility somewhere else? I mean, why hasn't he called her if he's alive?"

"That's what we want to find out, Pete. That's exactly what we want to find out," said Adam, trying to convince himself that what he was about to do was okay. "It's all about closure, Pete. Marin is just looking for a way to end that chapter of her life. It must matter a great deal, for her to bring it up with me, a total stranger."

"As long as that's all you want me to do. But why me? Why aren't you doing this on your own? Why don't you mail the stupid thing?"

Adam answered with a sheepish expression, "I want to go in person in case Tyler shows up, but the woman caught me following her. I think it's best if it wasn't me going to their front door."

Pete rolled his eyes and slapped both hands on the table, palm down. "You're crazy, man. Why didn't you just talk to her and ask her about her son?"

"I don't know! It happened so fast, and I wasn't sure what to say. She actually caught me following her while I was pretending I wasn't, and I felt like an idiot. But it's too late to worry about that now. I did what I did, and I can only move forward. So, will you do it?"

The expression on Pete's face told Adam that he would do it. The subtle contortion of his jaw was also saying that he wasn't very happy about it.

23

ADAM SPENT THE NEXT FEW DAYS PUTTING TOGETHER AN advertisement, looking for persons who would be willing to take part in a study to determine suitability for counselling with a person who has similar experiences in order to better treat specific concerns. He then went on to list the criteria, obviously speaking to Tyler alone. The paper also asked for therapists of such patients to come forward. He hoped that *if* Tyler was in fact there but was unsure whether to respond to the flyer, he might pass it to his therapist.

Even while composing this flyer, Adam felt like he was partly insane and that this was a ludicrous thing to be doing. He harboured many doubts as to whether this tactic would work. His parents had immediately disliked the idea. Pete had tried to dissuade him. Being Dutch, Pete was sensible. He was educated, hard working, and honest. He had distaste for petty strategies such as this. He would have knocked on the door, like Steve Henderson had suggested. Nonetheless, being tolerant and a good friend, he had agreed to help.

Adam picked Pete up at his home on the assigned morning. The car was quiet on the drive to the border, so Adam turned the radio louder, thinking it would help his friend relax. He cared a lot for Pete, and in some ways, he was feeling guilty about dragging him out here like this. In hindsight, he could have come alone. Had he run into the woman again, his purpose for being there would have been the same as Pete's. But it was too late now, and there would be no advantage to mentioning it. For such an educated man, he was certainly making some very empty-headed decisions.

Traffic was light, and it was dry and mild. The grey clouds were thick and ominous. It was a good day for deception. As they approached the neighbourhood, Adam was reminded of his last visit to the house, and he ran his hand through his hair trying to rub away the memory. When he got closer to the street, he turned left and slowed down. Adam pulled over to the side of the road. He was parked two blocks from the Murphy house. Reaching to the back seat, he grabbed a few flyers from the stack he had placed on the floor. He handed them to Pete and again gave him the house number.

"Just walk up to the door, stick it in the mailbox, or wedge it into the door, then leave. That's all you have to do." Just as Pete reached for the door handle, Adam looked at him and said, "Shit, Pete, take your sunglasses off. It's not even sunny out. You look like a thug."

After placing the sunglasses on the dashboard, Pete got out of the car.

* * * *

PETE LOOKED BOTH WAYS as he crossed the street and headed towards the house. With each stride, something inside him was screaming not to do this. As he was climbing the steps to the front door, it opened and there stood a big angry-looking man with unruly greying hair and a fleshy face. He wore a stained T-shirt and track pants. His feet were bare. Pete felt the blood drain from his face.

The man looked at him hard before speaking. "What do you want?"

Pete swallowed a huge lump in his throat and his voice came out a whisper. "We are d-doing some research on trauma patients."

The man stepped forward until Pete could feel the heat from his face. "So, what made you pick this specific house? I didn't see you go to the house next door."

"Well, funny you should ask that. Specifically, I wanted to ask you about your son. I had heard about him from an old colleague in Washington, and I thought he'd be good for this study." He stepped forward, hand outstretched, paper grasped firmly in hand. In a flash, Pete realized it may not have been wise for him to have said that and instantly stopped talking.

Suddenly the man's eyes were on fire. "Leave us alone. I don't know who you really are or who sent you, but get off my porch or I'll call the cops."

As Pete walked abruptly down the steps, he heard the door slam behind him. He muttered angrily to himself as he hurried down the sidewalk back to the car.

* * * *

ADAM WATCHED AS PETE WALKED down the street towards him, and he noticed the hurried way in which his friend was moving. As he neared the car, Adam saw the anxious expression on his face. Pete was just getting into the car when Adam heard someone calling out behind him. He turned to see a woman walking towards him from the rear side of the car. She looked back in panic, as if to make sure nobody would see her.

Seeing it was Adam in the car, she cried out, "It's you! I recognize you. You followed me. What do you want? More importantly, who sent you?"

Adam looked at her with genuine discomfort. "I can assure you without a doubt that no one has sent me, so I have no idea what you mean." Adam slowly handed her his card and one of the flyers before saying, "I really am a doctor. I'm doing research and I just want to talk to you about something very important."

She shook her head in apparent disgust as she turned and hurried back to the house. But before she did so, she had snatched the card and the paper from Adam's hand.

"Stick to being a doctor, Adam. You're proving to be a shit detective," said Pete, as he slumped in the seat and reached for his sunglasses, even though it wasn't sunny out, as Adam had previously pointed out.

Adam was clearly rattled. "What the hell happened back there?" he asked as he pulled away from the curb.

"The guy was home. He came outside and confronted me. I may have mentioned his son, or Washington or something."

"Please say you didn't."

Pete looked at him in surrender and said, "I'm afraid I did. The man went ape-shit on me. He asked me why I was going only to his house and not the neighbours. I didn't know what to say."

Adam, trying to reduce the tension in the car, could only say, "Well, I guess we didn't talk about that. It would have looked better if you went to a few other places as well. I guess we didn't figure on him being there and watching you out the window. You're right, Pete. I think I'll stick to what I do."

"What about her, though? Why would she come from behind and approach you like that?"

Adam answered, "I was thinking the same thing."

Pete was rubbing his hands together, either from the cold or nervousness, before he added, "She asked you who sent you. He asked me the same thing."

"It makes me think they are definitely hiding from something or someone. Maybe she does want to talk about it. She did take my card. I'll have to wait to see what she does with it.

"Let's hope it's not a bad thing that she took it. You don't want this to come back and bite you in the ass. Now she knows who you are and where you're from."

Adam said nothing, but Pete was right, and he needed to think the same thing. There could be very unpleasant implications.

Pete looked down at the dirty puddle around his feet and added, "Sorry about the slush. I didn't have time to knock it off."

Right now, slush was the least of Adam's problems.

24

ADAM WOKE EARLY AND MADE HIMSELF A COFFEE BEFORE making his way to the sofa in front of the fireplace. Sitting down, he opened his laptop and saw he had two new messages from Sofia. The first was a short message to say that she was nearing the end of the teaching semester, and although she had enjoyed it, she would not teach another. Her grandmother was improving, yet her mother didn't seem in a hurry to return to Canada. Sofia was happy to announce that she had enrolled in cooking classes and hoped to master the craft of the cuisine of this region. She planned to dazzle Adam with her newly found skills in the art of preparing tortellini, ribollita, and tigelle. And he would need to wait to find out what they were.

The other message was a series of photos that Sofia had taken of the area, including a few of her students, when she had taken them on an outing to the Cathedral of Modena and the Torre della Ghirlandina. She explained this was the Gothic bell tower attached to the cathedral. The duomo with the tower, she wrote, is designated as a world heritage sight.

Adam scrolled quickly through the pictures until he saw one of Sofia. And there she was, looking radiant, her white teeth gleaming in the sunlight, her black hair swept back in the breeze. She had perfect olive skin, and her eyes were the colour of espresso. In the photo, Sofia was posing with three of her students, all of them waving. He smiled warmly at the picture, acutely aware of her absence and his aloneness. Although her being in Italy was allowing him this diversion to go on his quest for Tyler, he still longed for her to return. He ran his finger over her face and smiled warmly.

Adam looked around the room where there were clear signs of a childless family. Expensive pottery placed precariously within the grasp of young curious fingers, candles on coffee tables, delicate potted plants, carefully placed decorative throws on chair arms . . . not one thing was out of place. But suddenly, and profoundly, it seemed to lack life. No children's books, or drawings tacked to the fridge. No puzzles, nursery songs, small art tables, or toys. And no play apparatus in the yard. Things needed to change when Sofia came home.

The days went quickly and already a week had passed since the fiasco in Buffalo. Adam had not spoken to Pete since then, and was wondering how his friend was doing. He was on Yonge Street, not far from home and it had just started to snow, the grey, swollen clouds finally surrendering their freight. Adam frowned. Winter shouldn't last this long.

All of a sudden, Adam's phone was pinging, but he was on the main road and didn't want to risk fumbling with his bag on the back seat. When he finally pulled over to retrieve it, he saw it was a message from Steve Henderson: "Wife's last name was Greene. The new business is registered as Greene Mechanical Contractors."

Adam was minutes from home, so as soon as he got in the door, he called Steve back.

"I've been to Buffalo, Steve, and we accidentally ran into him."

Steve responded by asking, "Who is 'him'? Do you mean Tyler? Describe accidentally."

"Accidentally meaning my friend went to his door and 'him' meaning Keith came outside. And you were right in saying he's not very approachable. My friend might have made a mistake by mentioning Washington."

Adam went on to explain what he had been trying to achieve by going there, and how badly it went, except for the fact that Barbara had followed Pete back to the car and did take Adam's card. "She recognized me from the last time I was there."

"Let's hope there's no repercussion for you," said Steve, although sounding somewhat unconcerned. It was, after all, not his problem.

"There was some sort of feud between the two families," he continued. "Tyler's dad, Keith, was involved with this group of guys who hung out at some house just outside of town. I am trying to determine whether or not Marin's dad, Geoffrey, was involved as well. As I mentioned, someone died there, but everyone denied any wrongdoing. All their statements pointed to it being an accidental death. The statements, I have been told, were conveniently similar, but with no evidence of whether they were fabricated, nothing could be done. There's another thing I found out, about the Mexican fellow. His name is Jose-Luis something or other. He's known to have ties to Mexico's powerful Sinaloa drug cartel, although they've never been able to pin anything on him. He appeared in the area about a year earlier and was definitely around at the time of that suspicious death. The rumour was that he was looking to recruit people to launder drug money."

Steve continued, "He's wanted for assault, but there was no way to prove any real connection to the Sinaloa Cartel. The man is very careful, so the money laundering so far is just speculation. But funny enough, there is a suspected link to KM CO. Contractors. That was Keith Murphy's company. So, I wouldn't be surprised if Jose-Luis had something to do with the death out at that house. Then, after the accident involving Marin's mother, this guy fell off the planet. Nobody could find him."

"So, is he a suspect in that? Are they looking for him actively?" as Adam spoke, he was holding the phone under his chin while he struggled to remove his coat. He was grateful to be inside and had no intention of leaving the house again today.

"They were always watching him, just waiting for him to slip up. But suddenly, he was nowhere to be found. He had apparently gone back to Guadalajara or somewhere."

Adam's heart was pounding. "I know they had ruled it as accidental, but do you think he could have killed Marin's mom?"

"I don't know how the case was left. The police could never link him to it, but like I said, he disappeared so nobody could ask him, either." Steve let out a sound that was a bit like a grunt, and then continued, "Oddly enough, Geoff Jackson's name was in the paper today. Someone tried to run him off the road, but the manoeuver backfired and the perp himself ended up getting badly hurt. He's in the hospital with a couple of broken arms. That should keep him in place for a while until we figure this thing out. The important thing is," Steve said with emphasis, "now I'm interested in this myself because I just found out the name of the guy that hit him."

"And?" Adam's curiosity was piqued.

"It was Jose-Luis."

Adam was excited. "So he came back. Do you think there might be a reason he hit Geoff, of all people, or do you think it was random? Why that particular car? That particular man? Or maybe he didn't try. Maybe it just was an accident?"

Steve replied, "Do you mean, after he maybe accidentally pushed Marin's mom Angie off a cliff?"

"Well, there's that." Adam thought for a minute then said to Steve, "Well, along that vein, do you think it had anything to do with us approaching Keith last week? The man really was acting strangely. And he asked Pete who sent him."

"I'm going to check out this dude in the hospital first. See if it is who I think it is. This thing has suddenly become bigger than a missing person."

Adam then said to Steve, "When I saw Keith's wife, she took my card. I wonder if she plans on contacting me? Maybe she feels a need to talk to someone. If she does, I might find out about Tyler. Maybe we can share information going forward."

This time, Steve agreed. "Keep in mind the police may come back into this one as well, particularly if they might finally have something on the guy. And they might be coming for Keith as well. Hopefully they can prove Jose-Luis actually did try to run Geoffrey's car off the road and why."

"I know there's probably no doubt, but will you let me know if that is the same Jose-Luis?"

"Yes," said Steve. "I will. Even though we would still need

something to connect them all."

Hanging up, Adam felt an overwhelming desire to drive back to Buffalo.

25

MARIN RAN INTO THE HOUSE, OUT OF BREATH. SHE'D HAD A breakthrough. She remembered something about her mother. It was just after she was moved to her new room at the hospital. For the first time in over a year, she finally wanted to call her dad. All day, Marin had anticipated making this call and had tried hard to get away early while everything was fresh in her mind.

The phone rang twice and was answered by her sister, Lauren, who asked, "Is this really you, Marin?"

At the sound of her sister's voice, Marin had a sudden longing to see her and to be at home. "Yes, it's really me. How are you? How's school?"

"I'm good, but it's freaky you are calling today. Dad's been in an accident. It happened yesterday. Luckily, it was nothing major. A car came at him, but it was the car that ended up further in the ditch than Dad, and the man was taken to the hospital. So, either someone had tried to run Dad off the road or it was just accidental that he drove right into Dad's car."

"Why didn't you call and let me know?"

Lauren slightly laughed. "It just happened yesterday, and I've just gotten home from the hospital. I've been in school all day. Besides, why would I think of it when you've made it clear you didn't want to be part of us? We didn't even hear from you at Christmas."

"Didn't you get my card?" As Marin said the words, she realized how pathetically lame it sounded.

"It was a card, Marin. Big deal. You didn't even put a letter inside to let us know how you are doing."

Marin knew she had no explanation, so carried on with her question instead. "So why were you at the hospital? Is Dad still in there? I thought you said he wasn't hurt?"

"They kept him overnight for observation, but he's coming out later this afternoon. They discharged him to me, and I'm picking him up shortly. Then I'm taking him to the shop. We'll be home later. Why are you calling?"

"I just wanted to talk to Dad. I've been remembering more things about after the accident . . . still trying to piece things together. Lauren, do you happen to remember a dark-haired man that Mom might have known?"

"Dark-haired? Anyone in particular? I'm sure she knew lots of people with dark hair. What's this about?"

"I remembered a man with dark hair talking to Mom. Actually, he was yelling at her, in the hall just outside my hospital room."

"I dunno, maybe it was a doctor? I wasn't around a lot then, Marin. I was only fourteen or something. Dad kept me away from the hospital, but I guess you wouldn't remember that, being in a coma and all."

"Can you get Dad to call me when he comes home? Please, Lauren, don't forget," said Marin, with emphasis.

"But don't you want to talk to me?" Her sister suddenly

sounded reluctant to hang up the phone. "How are you?"

Marin spent the next twenty minutes telling her sister about her life in Arizona. She hadn't realized how badly Lauren missed her, but it was slowly starting to sink in. Lauren had lost her mother at an important age and then lost Marin as well when she had moved away with scarcely a word. Lauren was left with an emotionally absent father and nobody to talk to, not to mention dealing with the grief of losing their mother.

Before Tyler had come along, Marin had spent a lot of time with her sister, although she realized for much of that time, Marin had been sneaking her mother's gin and was not always the best companion for her sister. Undeniably, their lives had improved since moving to Kirkland, but it seemed to bring a whole new set of problems. The biggest problem being Tyler and the odd attitude his family had when around her.

She could never figure out the distain Tyler's dad had felt for her and her family, notably her father.

"How's school, Lauren? Any plans for next year?" Lauren was the serious one, very studious and driven. The family always knew she would do well.

"Well, with you gone and Dad being weird, I didn't really have a lot of time to make plans. I've been here, Marin, looking after him and the house. I've had to take the place of Mom after you left, and it hasn't always been easy." There was no malice in her voice, just fact.

"You sound so grown up," said Marin, sitting back in her chair. She had started to relax somewhat, the urgency leaving her. "I do miss you, and it would be good to see you. I think I should take some time off and come home for a while. What do you think?"

Marin could feel the excitement in her sister's voice, and she squealed into the phone, "Yes, please! We'd love you to come home! When are you coming? Shall I tell Dad?"

Marin laughed. "I need to talk to my boss first and see what she says, but I promise, I'll call you in a few days and let you know when I'll be there." Before she hung up, she said to her sister, "Oh, Lauren? Yes, you can tell Dad I'm coming home."

It wasn't until she hung up the phone that she did realize how badly she wanted to go home. In spite of everything, she suddenly felt that going home might actually help her heal. She needed to face her demons head on, beginning at the source. Thinking she needed to go for a walk to clear her head, Marin headed towards the door and slipped on her shoes. Stepping outside, she was disappointed to see a monsoon rolling in. The dusty dry ground was now smattered with small rain craters that were steadily multiplying as the rain grew in intensity.

Coming back in the house, Marin decided she wouldn't be robbed of her good mood. She turned on the music loud, and went to the kitchen to open a beer and look for something to prepare for her dinner.

26

WEEKS HAD PASSED, AND ADAM WAS KICKING HIMSELF FOR bothering Steve Henderson, asking the man to come up with all the extra information regarding Keith Murphy's company. There was no way in hell he could ever approach the building or obtain any information regarding employees. Adam felt he should have saved up his favours on something that may have been a little more valuable. He would have to find another way to get his information. But this mysterious Mexican man intrigued him. He was anxious to see what more Steve could learn about him.

Adam also realized that it didn't mean he'd be any closer to finding out about Tyler. The incidents could very easily have no bearing on each other. He didn't want to lose his focus, which was, first and foremost, Tyler. Although busy at work, he did have a lot of spare time with Sofia gone, so he decided to go back to Buffalo at his earliest opportunity. It still didn't mean he'd know what to do once he got there.

The following week, Adam again found himself in Buffalo, parked in front of the same deli, only not quite as close. He sat in his car, staring off into space, hoping something would come to him, an epiphany, or something remotely close to a great idea.

Sitting still in his car, it wasn't long before he started to feel cold and cramped. At the same time, he became aware of activity near the intersection ahead of him. It began with a few people coming and going, and it progressed to the point where there was now a myriad of activity. People were walking around the corner alone but coming back with dogs.

Feeling a need to move, Adam climbed out of his car. It felt warmer outside than it had in his vehicle. He loosened his coat and headed down the street towards the activity. Approaching the intersection, it became clear what was going on. A large banner overhead announced that the local pet shelter was holding an adoption event. The traffic had been blocked down one lane to allow for the animals to be displayed along the sidewalk and roadway. Some pets, like rabbits and cats, were crated. Dogs were outside, leashed and held by volunteers. Adam was surprised at how many people were taking pets home with them. This was undoubtedly a great fundraiser for the small community shelter.

Adam stood watching for a short time. A portly woman in a dark-green parka had just adopted a tiny Shih Tzu puppy. As she paid her donation, she noticed that standing behind her was a little girl of about ten years of age, in tears. She had arrived seconds to late to buy the same puppy. The woman stood for a moment then began to walk away. She suddenly turned around and leaning down, gave the puppy to the starry-eyed youngster, who cried out in joy. Adam thought, if only life was always that easy.

Looking at his watch, Adam realized he should head back to his car. Nothing productive was happening here. Just as he neared the corner, he ran straight into a woman who had been walking quickly with her head down. As fate would have it, the woman was Barbara Murphy. He stood there looking at her in disbelief.

"Not you again," Barbara said, a startled look on her face. "I've seen you a few times now. You and your friend, the one with the flyer. Well, okay, I think if you were here to hurt us you would have done it by now. But who the hell are you and why do you keep coming back? What do you want?" She was looking up and down the street as if not wanting to be seen.

"Why on earth would I want to hurt you?" Adam was genuinely surprised by her comment. "My name is Dr. Adam Wyner, and I would really like to talk to you. It's about the flyer."

"Should I be afraid of you?" she asked.

Adam shook his head. "Of course not. I only want to talk. Can I buy you a coffee or something?"

"I'll talk to you if it will make you go away, but not here. I need to be at work in half an hour. I could have coffee with you there. It's a place near the freeway called Beatnik's Bistro. I'll meet you there because I need to go home first," she said, making a wide path as she made her way past him. She wore an expression similar to anger. Maybe not anger, Adam decided. Maybe annoyed. Yes, that was a better word. She turned around and added, "You really are pushy."

Adam found the bistro easily, and as he was walking in, he was hoping that Barbara wouldn't return with Keith, ready to beat him up or something worse. But as he walked in the door, he heard a car pulling into the parking lot. He turned and saw Barbara arriving alone. Adam waited to hold the door for her. She brushed past him without making eye contact or saying a word. She directed him to a table in the corner and then walked away. Barbara disappeared into the back and soon returned with two cups of coffee. Without asking if he wanted milk or sugar, she placed the steaming beverage in front of him and sat waiting. Adam removed his scarf and gloves and began speaking.

"First of all, Mrs. Murphy, I'm so sorry about your son."

She sat up in a panic. "Why? What's happened to Tyler? Isn't he at the shop this morning?" she started to get up.

Adam touched her arm. "No, I'm sorry, nothing is wrong. Please listen to me. I was talking about the accident in Washington. I, uh, I thought Tyler was dead."

Barbara stared at him, a strange expression on her face. "How do you know about Tyler? Who are you really?"

"I really am a doctor, and I really am concerned. Maybe just not in the way I said I was. You see, the truth is, I met Marin Jackson a couple of months ago and she told me—again, I'm sorry—but she told me Tyler was dead."

Barbara calmed down and sat back in her chair. She answered coldly, "What are the odds of you running into her then, being here in Buffalo? Are you from here? How did you happen to meet Marin?"

Adam's heart was pounding at the news that Tyler was alive. He felt euphoric but tried to remain calm. He apologized, although he wasn't sure why, then began to explain.

"I'm from Toronto and Marin is still in the west. She helped me out and I felt I owed her something, for what she did for me. You see, I had an accident and I don't know how well I would have survived if it wasn't for her. It's a long story. But she told me Tyler was dead, but she didn't know where he was. I wanted to bring her some closure or something." Adam's frenzied delirium was proving hard to disguise. He could barely contain his emotion, and he kept repeating to himself, *Tyler is alive*.

Barbara started to speak. "Why does she need closure? My husband, Keith, wants that life to go away. The truth is, he wanted everyone to believe that Tyler was dead. We thought it was more important for us to have our son alive than to stay there where it wasn't safe," she had come back with a forceful retort, as if somehow trying to defend their actions. She glared at him for a moment before adding, "So why the hell did you come to the house and mention Washington? Do you know what you might have done? And that also is a long story. Seems we both have long stories then."

"Well, we are here now. Can I get you another coffee? Or maybe some lunch?" Barbara had not moved, so Adam had taken that as a good sign.

"I told you, I'm here to work. I have no time for this right now."

"So, tell me about the accident. I thought I could offer to help your son in some way."

"My son almost died. He has his struggles but he's doing fine. He doesn't need any help from you."

"But why hasn't Tyler been in touch with Marin?"

The next words out of her mouth hit Adam like a punch in the gut.

"That will never happen because Tyler believes that Marin is dead."

The power of her words flooded his senses. He wasn't sure how to respond. It might be too easy to say the wrong thing and he would forever lose her. What was going on? Why would these two families want their kids to believe the other was dead? There was obviously something he was missing. Before he realized what he was doing, he asked Barbara, "Have you heard of a man called Jose-Luis?"

"Okay, conversation over. I can't sit here any longer. I have work to do," Barbara said, as she stood. "And you need to leave. Please don't come back."

Adam stood at the same time, but before he moved away from the table, he reached into his pocket and took out another one of his cards. "I'm going to leave this here, Mrs. Murphy, in case you decide to call me. I really think I can help your son."

27

ADAM WAS LESS CONCERNED WITH THE WAY BARBARA HAD pushed him out, as he was with the knowledge that Tyler was alive. This was very good news, and he felt quite triumphant—almost delirious. He wished he had someone to call at this moment to share the news. With a renewed sense of curiosity, Adam reached into his wallet and took out the piece of paper on which he had written the information Steve had given him. He left the restaurant, got into his car, and punched the address into his GPS. Within a few minutes, he was driving in to a small strip mall in an industrial area. On the end of the building was a big green door with a sign above that read Greene Mechanical Contractors. Barbara had said that Tyler was at the shop. Adam was assuming this was where she meant.

He parked at the far end of the small lot. Checking his watch, he noted it was nearly three o'clock. A few people were starting to emerge from the building. Not knowing what to do, he sat waiting to see who was coming and going. He contemplated going in and asking for Tyler, but then thought better of it. After twenty minutes had passed, the activity had dwindled, so he got out of the car and made up his mind that he would speak to the next person who came out of the building. It was a man of about the same age as Tyler.

Walking up to him, Adam began speaking nonchalantly, "Oh man, I'm late. I was supposed to meet Tyler Murphy here, do you know if he's left?" He was trying to look and sound cool and laidback.

"Nope," the man responded. "Today is Monday. He always leaves at two o'clock on Mondays; some doctor shit he goes to."

"I know, I was planning on going with him today," said Adam nervously. He knew he was not a good liar. "Do you know where the session is?"

The man shook his head. "I think it's some clinic over by the church, but I'm not sure."

Adam looked at his watch. It was twenty minutes to four. He was possibly too late, but at least, he could find where these sessions took place. Thanking the man, Adam walked back to his car.

He drove around the neighbourhood, in the general direction of the Murphy residence, until he found a church with a small annex. Parking his car near the annex side, Adam got out of his car and headed towards a large brick display sign. Many notices were posted on a cork bulletin board under glass. Sure enough, there was a schedule for weekly sessions. A men's PTSD clinic was being held each Monday at two fifteen in the afternoon. Adam walked to the building and tried the door. It was locked. He walked back to the display board to read the notice one more time. There was a contact number at the bottom of the page. Adam retrieved his phone out of his pocket and took a picture of the notice before heading back to his car.

Adam drove around the neighbourhood for a bit longer,

making sure there were no other churches in the area that held such meetings. Convinced he had the right place, he looked for the road to get him out of town.

The drive home was not appealing. He would be directly in the middle of rush hour and it could take him an extra hour to make the trip. However, Adam had no other option and was always happy to be leaving this place. If traffic turned out to be really bad, he would opt to stop in Hamilton and have an impromptu visit with Pete and Linda.

Each time Adam made this trip to Buffalo, he found that he made progress, however small. And each time, he came away with different takes on the situation. Today, he had heard troubling admissions.

The following day, Adam called the number on the corkboard and had left a message for a man named Dr. Denison. He stated his name and expressed his interest in sitting in on one of his sessions. He then left his number in case the doctor chose to return his call; however, he did also leave a date for which he hoped to return to Buffalo. Feeling inefficient, Adam spent the next few days digesting the conversation he had with Barbara Murphy. He felt powerless to do anything.

"So, Marin thinks Tyler is dead, and Tyler thinks Marin is dead," Adam had said to Barbara. He had squeezed his eyes shut before continuing, "This is unimaginable, that you could possibly think this is an okay thing to do!"

The woman had just sat there in silence. But thinking about it, Adam strongly believed something didn't sound right about the story. To move the family, sell your company and your home, and sneak out of town sounded like a pretty extreme measure just to keep two kids apart. There had to be more to the story. It might have had more to do with money laundering, murder, and one mysterious Mexican named Jose-Luis. Barbara had suddenly been in a hurry when Adam had mentioned the man.

* * * *

CLAIRE AND BEN SAT IN front of the fire. They both ached from their day of snowshoeing the backcountry around Rogers Reservoir. It had snowed all night, leaving an abundance of fresh fluffy white stuff. The weather was now clear, crisp, and sunny. Claire's cheeks still burned from the cold air. Sipping their coffee and rum, Claire turned to Ben and answered him. He had just asked her what she thought of Adam going down the same path that she was on, all those years ago.

"Well, you shouldn't be surprised that he's doing this. I mean, he's been trying to look after you since he was eight years old. He always felt it was his job to care for his dad because his mom had abandoned you. So, we know it's in his nature to help people. This has been his calling. It's what he's good at and what he thrives on."

"But this is different. This isn't part of his job, is it?"

Claire smiled, studying Ben's face. He wore a worried expression. "Hey, just think about it," she said, "Adam is a smart man. He's very different than me, and my case was very different from his. I think he will know when enough is enough, but he needs to try." Claire sighed. "Look, Ben, Adam is sensible and he's always been obedient. Maybe now he needs to be a bit disobedient. As a doctor, he may be truly concerned for this person's well being. He's trained to look for red flags—maybe he sees one somewhere. And you know that the more you show your displeasure, the more he'll get his back up. It may make him more determined if he thinks you disapprove."

Ben nodded in agreement. "As long as he doesn't get hurt. I wouldn't know what to tell Sofia."

28

ADAM'S HOME WAS NEITHER HUMBLE NOR EXTRAVAGANT, although it certainly had more square footage than was necessary given there was just the two of them. The houses, which sat on generous lots in the cul-de-sac, were all of similar architecture, tasteful and a cut above. A renowned developer, who had been keen to create something exceptional on this plot of land, had lovingly built the ten homes. He and Sofia had chosen tastefully neutral colours for the exterior, and their love of gardening kept ambitious yard maintenance companies at bay, their grounds being always well groomed.

Adam raised the garage door, and he threw his overnight bag into the trunk, feeling a twinge of remorse for the time he had been spending away from home. Getting into his car on this bright afternoon, Adam slowly backed out of his driveway and onto the road. Two of his neighbours were outside, having what appeared to be an affable conversation, their laughter echoing across the crisp air. Three small children were nearby, smashing piles of melting snow into slush with their boots. It was overcast, but mild. Patches of green were beginning to show here and there.

He paused to wave but didn't stop. He felt a bit embarrassed that he didn't know their names. If Sofia were here, she would be the one to stop and talk to them for a minute, to say hi and catch up. Adam had a strong focus on family, but he was a self-professed loner. It was never his thing to hang out in large groups. He preferred the company of a few. And although he loved his home and neighbourhood, it was not like him to wander over and involve himself in idle chat.

Even in sports, he leaned towards the individual ones, like skiing or cycling, staying away from organized team sports. This was just who he was, possibly from having grown up an only child. Adam loved his family and friends and felt a bond with his patients, but he was protective of his privacy. He saw enough of the public when he had need to.

Adam was looking forward to this weekend. He and Pete make this trip every year, usually with their wives, but as Sofia was in Italy, Pete's wife had chosen to let the men go alone. Their trip to Niagara-on-the-Lake for the annual Ice Wine Festival was one of the things that Adam enjoyed about the winter. This being a Friday, Pete had booked a room, so they could enjoy the opening festivities that evening while having the entire day on Saturday to do their tasting and Sunday to have a morning of recovery before returning home. Ben and Claire had plans to join them on Saturday for a few hours of tasting followed by lunch.

Adam had a clear head with no distractions and was smiling as he pulled into Pete's drive. Within seconds, Pete emerged, followed by Linda, who stood on the doorstep and waved. Adam jumped out of the car and went to give her a hug while Pete put his overnight bag in the trunk. Slapping Adam on the arm, Pete went to the doorstep to kiss his wife goodbye.

Soon, the men were on their way.

Driving past the turn-off to Niagara-on-the-Lake, Adam chose to exit further ahead to drive through the town of Niagara Falls. It was an impulsive move. He hadn't been to the actual town for at least twenty-five years, since he was a just a kid. His heart sank as he drove through Clifton Hill. What was once magical and intriguing to a child now looked worn and tattered, the midway having seen better days. King Kong was still perched atop the fallen Empire State Building at Ripley's Believe It or Not, causing Adam to smile. The casinos, souvenir shops, arcades, and haunted houses looked almost vulgar and outdated. With new awareness, he winced at this now seedier side of town. He watched questionable-looking people loitering on street corners, cigarettes hanging out of their mouths, exchanging things out of their pockets with other dubious-looking people. He also noticed what seemed to be a growing homeless issue, as he spotted bodies under blankets in doorways.

But the memories of this place as a child still held his heart. One of his favourite childhood adventures had been the boat ride, where, donned in yellow raincoats, they would be herded like cattle into the Maid of the Mist. The boats then motored out into the water, dangerously close to the heart of Horseshoe Falls, covering everyone with the mist and foam from the powerful cascade of water.

Passing through the end of the town, Adam had seen enough. Pulling on to the Niagara Parkway, the two settled in for the scenic drive back to Niagara-on-the-Lake.

Adam and Pete were staying at a hotel near the historic old town. After checking in, it wasn't long before they were walking down the street to have their dinner. It was dark, and they were tired, but the fresh air and brisk walk brought them back to life. The atmosphere was spirited and invigorating, and it made Adam forget about the cold, to which by now he had re-acclimated. Arizona seemed like years ago. They made their way to a tapas bar, where they sampled a variety of dishes and drank copious amounts of good local wine. He had no idea what time it was when he finally fell into his bed.

On Saturday, after a morning of coffee and newspapers, they made their way to meet Ben and Claire and begin their exploring before retreating into the Charles Inn for a late lunch at the HobNob. This building, having been erected around 1832, had been beautifully restored, with elegant arched door-ways and crown molding. While the hotel was an expensive place to stay, this restaurant was a favourite with locals and tourists alike, with the white tablecloths and its down-home extravagance, if you will. Claire loved the menu and was never disappointed. Today, their table overlooked the street, where they could observe the activity from the coziness within.

Adam had talked about the trains he and Pete had seen yesterday while driving from Niagara Falls, and now Ben was talking about how as a child, Adam would listen to the trains at night. Often, they would wake him up on a hot summer night when the windows were wide open.

Adam laughed and said, "But what you didn't know was, as I lay awake for what seemed like forever, I used to imagine the people on it. I would make up stories of who they were and where they were going. At times, they were elaborate stories, depending on how long it took me to fall asleep. And they all had problems, and I would try to solve them."

"You never told me that before," said Ben.

"I guess over the years I forgot about it, until just now." Adam loosened his scarf, the food and wine having warmed him. Turning to Claire, he asked, "Do you remember that song you used to sing me all the time when I couldn't fall asleep?"

She nodded and smiled. "Oh yes, that was a song you really loved. It was 'Moscow Nights.' 'Podmoskovnye Vechera.'"

"Yes! That's it!" Adam laughed out loud. "*'Not even a whisper is to be heard in the garden, everything has calmed down until dawn. If you only knew how dear they are to me, the Moscow evenings!'* It was a love song, wasn't it?"

Claire was quiet as she nodded. It was bringing back memories of her grandparents.

"But there is something else I'd like to talk about, if nobody minds. I want to ask you all about love. More specifically, about this theory of love at first sight. I want to know if you believe in such a theory."

His father, Ben, was the first to answer. "I know you have been thinking about that lately because of this couple Marin and Tyler."

Adam turned to him and said, "I have been speaking to people at work, and I asked them about the love-at-first-sight concept, or soul mate, or a belief in destiny. It's surprising how many people do believe."

Claire was looking at her soup. She picked up her spoon, and then put it down again. This was one conversation she would prefer not to get involved in. Her thoughts were of Oliver, but she didn't utter a word. Claire was one who believed in it.

Pete spoke up, which was unusual for him. "My wife, Linda,

was my second serious girlfriend, but I never thought about it beyond just falling in love with her. I have no intention of leaving; I love her and that's that. There's no special formula for anyone. I think it's what works for you."

Claire partially agreed. "I remember what my dear friend Wolfgang had said about his wife, Ilse. He called her his *seelenverwandte*, his soul mate. He said he had known the minute he had laid eyes on her that he would never be with anyone else."

Adam nodded in agreement. "I have a colleague who said almost the same. He said the first time he laid eyes on his wife, it was an instant physical attraction, followed very closely by an instant feeling of love and wanting to protect her. He believes that love isn't something you see, it's deeper, from inside."

Ben crossed his legs and sat back in his easy chair, stroking the armrest absentmindedly. He smiled inwardly and looked at his son. "I think it was like that for you, Adam."

Adam agreed. "I knew I wanted to take care of Sofia forever, and I couldn't imagine doing anything else. But the first attraction was definitely her physical appearance." He smiled and blushed. "I think if she had refused me, I'd have gone on loving her forever."

Now Claire spoke. "I believe you. And I think what your friend Marin says is true, Adam. It's like the Titanic song. Love can touch us once and it can last for a lifetime. And it won't let go until you die."

Ben shook his head in disagreement. "But that's just a song."

Claire let out a sigh. "Yes, but songs are written about peoples experiences, so it's about life, and it then becomes a song."

Turning to Adam, Ben then said, "I love Claire, I always

have, since we first met. But I loved your mom, too."

"But she walked out on you and hurt you," said Adam, a bewildered look on his face.

"That's true, but I still loved her. I just didn't like her much anymore. I'm just not sure I believe in this theory of only one person made for another."

"You don't have to believe it, Dad; maybe just acknowledge that it might exist. Maybe not for everyone, but it does exist."

Pete, chuckling, then said, "I can't imagine that man Keith falling for that, by the looks of him. There seems to be nothing pleasant about that guy."

Ben turned to Pete and asked, "Do you mean the man in Buffalo? When did you see him?"

Pete looked at Adam. "Oops. Cat's out of the bag, man."

Ben and Claire exchanged glances before both staring back at Pete, who proceeded to tell the story of the flyer. Adam leaned back in his chair, his face buried in his hand.

"This is the flyer you agreed not to hand out?" Ben looked at his son in disbelief, as if his son had suddenly become unrecognizable.

"It was too late; we'd already done it before we spoke about it," was all Adam could offer.

Claire berated Adam. "You could have got him killed, sending him out like that. What were you thinking?

Before they ganged up on him and had him beheaded, Adam decided to explain his scheme about the flyer to Ben and Claire.

Ben was agreeing with Claire. "And what would happen when you needed to produce this so-called patient?"

"I could say he dropped out unexpectedly. It happens."

Ben threw his hands up in surrender. "Seems like you've thought of everything."

"Is it ethical?" asked Claire.

"Well, everyone seems to think it's not. Everyone but me. I am not using this information for any devious purpose. It's just a back door to the truth."

With three sets of eyes glaring at him, Adam at last acquiesced. "Okay, it didn't work. So, I'll go to the clinic and to be sure, I'll wait in the car until I see Tyler go in, if I can recognize him. I can't go for the next two weeks, but I'll go by the end of the month." Adam then told the three about his encounter with Bonnie and what she had said, how both Marin and Tyler believed the other was dead, and that it was for the best.

"It's kind of like *Romeo and Juliet*, don't you think? Not that I want to augment the tragedy side of it," said Claire. "But we have two feuding families and two star-crossed lovers who got caught up in their family dispute, each of whom now believes the other is dead." She shifted in her chair to face Adam. "Just be careful how you handle it. Make sure you know what you will say to him and be ready to deal with his response. Think before you act. Don't send the poor boy on some wild goose chase if you don't even know where the girl is."

Pete looked at Adam apologetically. For a moment, no one knew what to say. Claire wanted to get by this so they could continue enjoying their day.

She suddenly stood up. "Okay, I'm going to take some pictures. The light is perfect, and it's not too sunny. I will see you boys outside. Just walk through the park, towards the water. I'll be there." With that, she was gone.

Ben then turned to Adam and asked, "Have you spoken

with this girl Marin?"

Adam answered that he had no idea where Marin was. He needed someone to think he was acting sensibly, but that didn't seem to be the case here.

"Are you kidding me?" Ben's voice was a bit louder than he meant. With an apologetic look on his face, he cleared his throat and made an effort to sit back and look relaxed.

"But I know where she will be in April, on Tyler's birthday. I'll find her at Romero Pools. And besides, she's not the issue here, Dad. Tyler is. I want to know he's okay."

"So, what if she gets hit by a bus and doesn't show up? What will you tell him then?" Without waiting for an answer, Ben added, "Be careful how involved you get."

Adam looked at his dad strangely. "But what about what you taught me? About how it takes a village?"

Ben shot back, "But this is not your village. Is your village the entire continent?"

Adam looked his dad in the eye and answered, calmly and evenly. He knew his dad had a systematic mind, and Adam needed to sound very rational. He couldn't succumb to emotion. "She became my village the day she took me off the mountain, Dad. She trusted me and put herself at risk. I could have been anybody. I could have been faking my injuries, and I could have harmed her out there in the middle of nowhere. She placed blind trust in me the same way I did in her."

29

MARIN SAT IN THOUGHT. HER THERAPIST HAD JUST POSED A question to her, regarding the deaths of both Tyler and her mother: Did they each have the same impact on her?

"My mom alienated me at an early age, and I guess now I'll never know why. Sure, it was hard losing her, and I was tormented that there had been no chance for reconciliation. What's interesting, though, is that I suffered major trauma at the loss of Tyler. The news of his death sent me reeling. My mom and I were only connected through blood, whereas I will always struggle with intense loss and loneliness for that someone who was, well, an extension of myself. Tyler and me, we were meant to be."

The therapist looked at Marin. "We become separated from the people we know and who know us, and we lose the essence of who we are. But we can find it again."

Marin looked at her. "You know, sometimes I'll be walking down the street feeling really alone and then I'll pass someone and we'll make eye contact, and it's like, bam, we both 'get it'. And we look at each other with a kind of familiar knowing, and the essence comes back. But it's fleeting. We smile a knowing smile to each other and keep walking. It only lasts for that moment. So, I guess it's in there somewhere."

"Did you have a chance to say your goodbye to Tyler? Maybe you need closure," suggested the therapist.

"I can't describe what it felt like. I mean, I woke up but still had a long road ahead of me with recovery. I was in the hospital for what felt like an eternity. Then I was finally discharged and I had more rehab. But I remember the day my dad drove me past Tyler's house. It was creepy. The house was empty; the grass over-grown. There was a SOLD sign on the lawn. I asked about a grave, my dad told me there wasn't one. Perhaps he had been cremated and they took the ashes with them. But there was no obituary in the paper. And nobody seemed to know where the family went."

Marin took a sip of her water before continuing, "Then there was my mom. What is this crap about accidental death? Was it suicide or murder? Why would she want to kill herself? Why did it seem as if nobody was bothered to find out? Why was no one talking about it? What's scary is that my dad never spoke of it. I know it was hard for him, but didn't he know it was hard for me, too? I mean, my dad was by my bedside until I recovered. My sister came occasionally, but she was just a kid and all she did was cry. Anyway, once I was out of the hospital and doing therapy from home, everything kinda went back to normal. My dad acted like none of the events had taken place. How on earth was I expected to get back to any sense of normalcy with two deaths hanging over my head? I couldn't figure out what was going on. My dad never once asked me how I was doing. It was like nothing even happened. Bang—there went the end of the love and support. To me, it seemed like he didn't want to know me anymore. I don't know if he somehow blamed me for my mom's death. Nothing about it made any sense. Anyway, I didn't need him, either."

"It seems odd that both deaths ended in mystery. Do you completely trust your recollections of both?" The therapist spoke slowly, seeming hesitant to ask this.

"Well, nobody has told me I've got it wrong. But I try not to dwell on it anymore. My life is good. I mean, I love my job and I have some great friends. But I don't understand people who think I need a man in order to have love, to survive. I have lots of love around me. And Tyler is always with me. I was only seventeen when we met. We had the same group of friends, and we liked hanging out together. It just progressed from there, and we noticed that we just wanted to be together. It's true that at that age, you don't really think about it too much, but it just happened. One day, we looked at each other and I just knew. We dated seriously after that. Who knew me better? We grew up together, and he really helped me. Tyler was what I had been missing. He made me want to try harder, be better. And he did it all without saying a word. He gave me goose bumps, like a little kid, but he also made me grow up".

"So, where do you go from here, Marin?"

Marin sat in a near catatonic state, staring at the floor lamp that stood by her chair. Where does she go from here? What happened to her life? What happened to the days where she would wake up, dress, and run downstairs to greet her family? Kiss her dad as he headed out for work and thank her mom for making her lunch as she hurried her little sister along to drop her off at school on her way to classes. Where were the birthday parties, and Christmas mornings around the tree, waiting eagerly for the distribution of the gifts, their faces glowing with wonderment? She could hear her dad scream as she and Lauren pounced on him at the crack of dawn on his birthday. What did she do wrong to have made things turn out so badly? Why did this happen? Why? Why?

"Marin?" Her counsellor was talking to her. "Are you all right?"

Marin sat upright and suddenly seemed radiant. "You won't believe this, but I want to go home. I spoke with my sister, and she told my father. They want to see me, too. As soon as I can figure it out with my boss, I want to go for a few weeks or more, to see my family. I have been remembering more about the time of the accident, and I need to speak to my father. I'm hoping this can bring some closure for me, in regards to both my mother and to Tyler. I need this, and I feel ready to deal with it."

30

MARIN WAS NOW SEATED ON THE PLANE THAT WAS TAKING her home to Washington. She remained somnolent, almost comatose throughout much of the short flight, all of a sudden questioning her decision to return to the place that had brought so much sorrow. The sound and motion of the plane hitting the ground jolted her back to the now. Walking into the terminal, she searched the faces in the crowd until she spotted her father, appearing fresh and all smiles. Beside him stood her sister, looking very grown up. Marin walked up to her dad, and they greeted one another in a warm embrace. Her sister, Lauren, stood silently, and when it was her turn, she awkwardly hugged Marin.

As she expected she would, Marin felt distressed and out of place being here. On the drive to the house, she sat looking out the window as her sister prattled on. Nothing looked the same. Everything seemed smaller, dirtier, more congested.

When her dad pulled into the driveway, Marin wasn't sure she wanted to get out of the car. Once inside their house, Marin remained seated like a guest, feeling detached. It didn't seem to be her place to roam freely around the house. The tone of their conversations suggested ineptitude, their voices crippled, the words strained, unsure how safe it was to discuss certain things.

They hadn't been home long before her father ordered food from a local Chinese restaurant. Geoffrey went to fetch the food while Lauren set the table. He returned in no time, Marin thinking the restaurant must be very close to home. She sat in her customary place at the table, acutely aware of the empty place where her mom once sat. While her dad ate, he made little eye contact.

Marin used this time to study his face. He was a good-looking man, still quite young and handsome. She wondered if he planned on meeting anyone and getting on with his life. Or perhaps he had done, and was keeping it hidden. Something about his face reminded her of George, although he would need a lot of cheering up in order to really look like George.

It was after nine when Marin announced she was retiring. Kissing her father and sister, she headed down the hall to her old room. Her dad had dropped her suitcase there on the bed, but this was the first time Marin had ventured to this part of the house. She stood in the doorway and took in the room, feeling like she was in another world looking down on a past life. She felt weird being there; it was as if she was intruding on someone else. Here were all the remnants of a life gone by - a haunting reminder of a different Marin. Wondering if she would even sleep, she miraculously did. So soundly, in fact, that she slept late.

Looking outside, the day was sunny, but the thermometer showed her how cold it was. Marin spent the day with a big blanket wrapped around her shoulders. She did very little. She and Lauren watched some television programs, after which she wandered around the house looking at things she had forgotten about. Her father had gone to the shop for a few hours, promising not to be away for very long. That evening, although it was cold outside, they had a barbecue. Her dad had wheeled the grill onto the back porch, within inches of the door Lauren was reminiscing about how she and Marin would go everywhere on their bicycles and how Marin stopped riding hers after she met Tyler.

"You seemed to forget that you had a sister."

Marin bumped shoulders with her sister jocularly, saying she didn't quite remember it that way. "The way I remember it is that your friends would tease you for riding your bike when they all rode the bus."

"Maybe the other truth is that you were drunk half the time," Lauren retaliated.

Marin blushed and half smiled. "Well, there is that. But you need to understand that moving to Kirkland was extremely difficult for me. I was at an age where friends were very important to me. I got here and all my friends were left behind, and it was hard. Nobody at school wanted to know me, and we had no people my age in the neighbourhood. Mom was emotionally absent." Marin looked around to be sure her dad was still out back tending to their meal and out of earshot. "And I didn't know how to handle it."

Lauren looked at her sister and said, "You are much nicer now. You are like a different person. You are calm and pretty and you look really good!" Her smile was unaffected and heartfelt. Marin reached over and squeezed her hand.

The following day, Lauren returned to school, allowing Marin and her dad an opportunity to talk freely. But again, he first needed to go to his office to set up his appointments for the rest of the week. It had rained every day since that first sunny day, and Marin had forgotten how depressing the weather could be. As children, their dad would take them to the park in the rain, saying water would never kill them.

This was the first time that Marin was alone in the house, and she didn't like it. The walls seemed to be talking to her, and some not very nice memories were returning. Marin pictured her mother, moping about in a brooding fashion, observing Marin but not saying much. Marin thought about the booze-filled closet, wincing at the memory. She turned up the radio and tried to keep busy cleaning up the kitchen.

Sighing with relief, Marin at last heard her father come through the door. She followed him into the living room to ask if he was ready to talk. He sat down in a drab faux-leather chair that showed obvious wear in an otherwise cheerfully decorated room. Not waiting for an answer, Marin sat down beside him. Enough time had gone by, and she sorely wanted to go home to Tucson.

"I clearly remember a man at the hospital with Mom. He had dark hair, and he was yelling at her. Did you know him? He didn't look like a doctor."

"To give you an answer, I need to back up a bit," said Geoffrey, his hands uncharacteristically resting in his lap. Marin's father proceeded to tell her what he knew. Mostly, that Tyler's dad, Keith, hung around with some, what he described as, very dubious characters. They used to meet at someone's old house out in the country. He didn't know what they did out there, and he didn't really care, but then there was a death. The media were calling it a suspicious death, and the story was in the papers for weeks. The biggest concern lay with the testimonies of the men who were there. Each of their stories was ironclad, almost word for word, and not one of them ever altered a word, like they had some sort of pact, so nobody was ever charged.

"Did you know the man who died, Dad?" questioned Marin.

"His name was in the paper, but no, I didn't know him. He had a small renovation company, which I had never heard of." Geoffrey went on. "It had long been rumoured that the people at this house had a connection to a Mexican cartel, through a man named Jose-Luis. It was Angie, your mom, who had heard more details about the death. She said it wasn't an accident, and that she knew a relative of the deceased who swore he'd been forced into involvement with the Mexican, and with Tyler's dad, Keith."

"Is that the man I saw at the hospital? He seemed angry, like he was in her face yelling at her. What was that all about?"

"I'm getting there, Marin. Then when your mom saw me with Keith's wife, she was worried that I was involved as well. Your mom, not being the shy type, had driven by that house many times and, on one occasion, had spotted them. The Mexican guy had been standing outside talking to Keith, and they both saw her as she tried to turn the car around quickly to leave. I think she was trying to catch me there, but it back-fired." Marin's father sat with his shoulders hunched, his brow tight, his lips pursed.

"Is that the man I saw with mom at the hospital?" Marin asked again. "Why would he be there yelling at mom? And why were you talking to Tyler's mom?"

Seeing her dad tremble, Marin added, "Are you okay, Dad?"

as she reached over and squeezed his hand.

"Yes, I'm okay. I'm just trying to remember how it happened," he said, then continued, "Keith came to see your mom after the sighting out at the house. He said it would be a shame if any of us got hurt. Angie then made the mistake of mentioning 'that poor dead man,' saying she knew what was going on. She didn't, of course, but she was feisty, like you. She didn't like being threatened, and she didn't like Keith."

Marin tried to be patient as she waited for her dad to get to the point, yet she really wanted to hear this story.

"Tyler's mom, Barbara, came to see me just before they moved away. Tyler wasn't doing too well. He was still in a coma, and the doctors had to remove his leg."

Hearing this, Marin let out a cry and hugged her legs up to her body in fetal fashion.

"Tyler was being moved to Chicago, to one of the best brain trauma facilities. They were leaving right away. Apparently, Keith was just leaving everything behind, dissolving the company and leaving the house empty. Barbara was distraught."

"But why would Barbara come and tell you that, Dad? What aren't you telling me?"

"Apparently, Keith caught up with mom one day in town and told her to stay the hell away from his family and to keep her mouth shut. It was maybe a few weeks later that your mom noticed the Mexican man showing up wherever she went."

"Why would Mr. Murphy tell her to stay away from Tyler?" asked Marin. She could hear herself shouting. "Goddammit, Dad, just tell me."

With that, Geoffrey stood and left the room.

31

Marin followed her dad to the kitchen where he had just plugged in the kettle. She walked to his side and placed her hand gently on this arm.

"I'm sorry, I don't mean to be impatient." She spoke in almost a whisper."

"I'll get to it if you just let me tell the story my way." He threw his hands up in exasperation.

"Okay, let's get some tea and I'll make a sandwich, and we can try again," said Marin, in apology.

Plates in hand, they sat across from each other at the kitchen table, her dad in his usual chair by the window.

Geoffrey almost sobbed as he suddenly broke down and told Marin the whole story, from the beginning, about him and Barbara in college and how in love with her he had been.

"It was such a long time ago. I did love her, maybe the same way you say you love Tyler. But I guess she didn't love me the same way. After nearly a year together, she had apparently started hanging around with Keith. Well, she said he started coming around to where she worked. She had a part-time job to help pay for school. I saw them together one day. I didn't know why, but she just stopped talking to me. I had no idea what I'd done, or what had changed. Next thing I knew, I heard they were getting married. Apparently, a hasty marriage at that, which told me everything I needed to know. I drove by the church on the day of the wedding because I didn't want to believe it was really happening. And they moved away, end of story."

Marin sat in silence, a wave of nausea sweeping over her. She couldn't picture her dad with Tyler's mom, however long ago it was. This came as such a shock. She wondered if Tyler had known this. Could this explain his father's hatred for her, and her family?

Geoff looked at the expression on his daughter's face and added, "I was only nineteen when I dated Barbara. I thought I was in love, and for me, she was going to be my forever. My Barbie. When she did what she did, I became, understandably, very jaded. So, you can appreciate why I acted like I did when you, at nineteen, professed that Tyler was the one. 'Your life,' you called him. All I could think of was what had happened to me. I figured at that age you were still too young to know."

"But then you met Mom. She was only nineteen, and you were twenty-one. That's still young. And you must have felt that with her—what I feel with Tyler."

Her dad shook his head. "No, I didn't. I mean, I loved her and we married and settled down. It was secure and safe, but it was never fireworks. I decided that stuff is not real, and with Barb, I told myself I was just too young to know it."

"Well, sorry, Dad, but it can be real. Tyler still is my everything." Marin stood up. "Dad, I need to get some more tea and wash my face. Please don't go anywhere; we need to finish this."

Marin's hands were shaking as she filled her cup. She could hear her dad sighing behind her where he sat. Already, she could feel herself feeling saner. Many questions were being answered as to everyone's behaviour. She was not crazy after all.

After splashing some water on her face, Marin returned with her tea. Sitting down at the table, she continued, "So did Mom know all of this when you met her?"

"No, she didn't. It was only about five years ago, when I moved the family here to Kirkland, that it all came out. I had no idea that Barb and Keith lived here." Marin's father was hitting the table hard with his fist. "I remember I was in town that day and I heard my name being called. I turned around, and there was Barb. I just stood there, frozen in the spot where I stood. I barely recognized her; she had changed a great deal. She asked me to go for coffee, and I said yes. It was that day I learned more about what happened."

Marin saw her father as someone else at that moment. She envisioned him as a young man with a broken heart. She had no plans to interrupt him anymore; the man already looked disheartened.

"On the day that Barbie and Keith were married, I had parked across the street in my truck. I had to see it for myself. I remember watching them walk out of the church. There were very few people attending, a few of the girls threw handfuls of confetti on them. Then Keith looked up and saw me parked there. He leaned over and whispered something to Barb, then he flipped his finger at me, a snarl on his face. I started the truck and drove away. That was the last time I thought about her, or them. But Barb said that after I showed up at the wedding, Keith went mad, and for years after that, he accused me of fathering Tyler."

Marin froze in her chair. Was this possible? Was Tyler her brother? "So, she told you all of this over coffee? Was it true, Dad?" Marin didn't hide her distress; she wasted no time in getting right down to it. "Did she?"

"I wasn't comfortable rehashing everything. I didn't need to know any of this. But then, Keith spotted us coming out of the coffee shop. He recognized me, and he went ballistic. Stupidly, I met her one more time, just after you started seeing Tyler. She said she needed to tell me something important."

"And what was so important that you had to see her again, Dad? What did you think you owed her?" Marin cried.

"When you became involved with Tyler, Keith flew into a rage and forbid him from seeing you. Tyler, apparently, told him that wasn't going to happen. Barbara wanted to know if I had any power to break you two up, but I didn't want to involve your mom. I was already sorry that I knew this much."

"Just tell me if it's true, Dad. Is Tyler my brother?" asked Marin, feeling faint.

Marin's dad cleared his throat. "Of course, it's not true, Marin. There was nothing sexual between Barbie and myself back then. But then Keith went to see your mom and told her that I was the father of Tyler and that he had been seeing me and Barbara together, and he felt your mom should know what's been going on with her husband behind her back."

"This does explain a lot," Marin muttered to herself.

"It was only after your car accident that Keith suddenly switch gears, and his goal seemed to shower love on his only son and to keep him away from everyone. I was afraid that he had somehow caused the accident, to ward you off. I might have mentioned that to your mom, which set her off against Keith with new energy."

Marin shuddered. Her mom was indeed tenacious, but it was a foolhardy move.

Her dad continued, "So, she went to Keith's business, despite her being warned not to go near the place. She told him it was him that should leave her family alone, said she was going to call the cops and spill the beans about 'the murder,' as she called it. Then Barbara came to see me, and just like that, the Murphys were gone."

Marin didn't know what to say. She had a lot to process. How could they have not told her this? Her distress was turning to anger.

Geoffrey continued, "The next time your mom saw the Mexican get close to her, she gave him the finger and told him to piss off. I don't know if she suddenly felt braver with the Murphys having gone, or if she'd just had enough. Only then did she come home and tell me everything, about how she had been stalking Keith and how she was caught at the farmhouse."

"Dad, this is crazy! Why didn't I know any of this?"

"There would have been nothing to gain by telling you, Marin. You were young. So, I told your mom to stay out of it and to not go near Keith again. Your mom didn't speak to me for a couple of days after that. Finally, one night, we talked about Barbara and Tyler. I had no idea that Keith had spoken to her about it. She thought I had been doing something behind her back." Geoffrey's face changed expression. Marin noticed at that moment, he looked more collected, almost peaceful. "I walked away from her, too angry to have the conversation."

Geoffrey stood up and walked to the sink, where he stood with his back to Marin.

"Not long after that, maybe a day or two, I finally broke down and told her the whole story. It was that night, with you and Tyler both in the hospital, that I chose to convince her that I had no interest in Barbara or her family. That night, we started to fix something that I should have fixed a long time ago. She believed me when I said Tyler was not my son. I think she always believed it, but she needed to hear it from me. We were on our way to healing. But the next day, she was dead."

Marin sat quietly smoldering. Her mother was a warrior, trying hard to protect her dad and her, but she was never told. All these years, she had no inkling about what had been going on. Why so many secrets? After all, she had a big role in it. And it certainly explained her mother's drinking.

"Before your mom's funeral, this Jose-Luis showed up in front of our house. He just stared at me long and hard, then slowly drove away. That's the last time anyone saw him, so I guess he was never linked to the death of your mom. But by then, Keith's house was already empty and Tyler had long been transferred out of the hospital."

"So that was the man I saw yelling at mom in the hospital." Marin's mystery was solved. "And that's the man who you had the car accident with, isn't it, Dad?"

Her dad nodded. "Yes, it's the man who collided with my car a few days ago. I guess he had a reason to come back."

Her dad continued with the rest of the story. By the time Marin got out of the hospital, everything was over. Her mom was dead, Tyler's family had moved away, and her dad was afraid to mention anything about it to Marin or anyone. He had not objected to Marin moving away. He actually encouraged it, agreeing that she needed a fresh start. The truth was, he was afraid for her and didn't want her to stick around. He told nobody where she went. He explained to Marin that it was never because he didn't love her; he didn't want anyone to find her.

"But, Dad, you have to call the police! Today! Right now, while he is in the hospital. He can't hurt you now."

"But he'll have friends, and it's no secret where I live."

"But the police will likely grab him now anyway because of what happened. He's in the hospital! They know where to find him! And he won't make a run for it. The man can't go far, not alone and not with two broken arms. Maybe this stuff will come out on its own, but you can at least tell them what you just told me."

Geoff said to Marin, "What rips me apart is all these years, she thought I had feelings for Barbara. Although I told her that was just crazy, a small part of her may have thought Keith was telling the truth. She knew I had dated Barb before I met her and she thought I still loved her. But the truth is, I loved your mom. Barb showed her true colours back when we were nineteen. For me, it ended there. I should have tried harder to let Mom know how I felt."

Marin hugged him and cried. "I'm sure she knew, Dad."

Geoff spoke in a whisper now. "In the months following her death, I know things were disastrous, although I don't know how much of it you remember. Plus, you had your own issues, recovering, and hearing the news about Tyler.

The room was silent until Marin said, "I hated her, you know. For years. She was so detached, and I thought she hated me, too. If only she'd let me in. If I knew what was going on, I could have supported her. We could have supported each other."

Her dad seemed to be focused on the curtain, which was circling over the blowing heat register.

"Do you know what, Dad? We've had too many secrets for too long. I say, no more." She walked over to where he stood and, reaching over, grabbed his hand.

After a few minutes, Marin said, "Remember when you used to take us to the Oregon sand dunes? And sometimes you took mom over the big hills really fast, and she'd scream?"

Marin's dad smiled, and a reminiscent, heartening look came over his face.

Marin paused before adding, "Do you know where they are, Dad? The Murphys?

"I was kind of hoping they left the planet," he added, attempting a smile.

Swallowing the lump in her throat, Marin asked, "And do you know if he's alive?"

Her dad looked at her with genuine curiosity. "If who is alive?"

"Tyler." She could see that he was confused and that his answer would be the truth.

"I have no idea, honey. We were told he didn't make it. What makes you think otherwise?"

Marin shook her head. "Nothing, I guess. Anyway, forget it. Let me get us something better to eat. We are both exhausted. What's in the fridge?

"You won't be impressed," was his reply.

"Okay, change of plan," said Marin as she grabbed her coat from the hook.

"Where are you going," asked her dad, looking over at her.

"I'm going to the grocery store. I want to cook for you."

"You don't know how to cook," answered Geoff, surprise in his voice.

"Things change, Dad," Marin said as she mimicked a smile. She knew she would not sleep tonight.

32

ADAM SAT IN HIS CAR THAT HE HAD PARKED IN FRONT OF the church, at the community hall side. The building was annexed onto the church, and the entrance was only partially visible behind the overgrown bushes. The walls themselves were covered in moss and ivy, seeming to hold the crumbling bricks in place. The windows were partially obscured by the rampant ivy. The building looked sullen and cheerless in contrast to the brilliant blue of the sky and the stark white clapboard of the church.

Adam had arrived while the group was in session. There were about ten minutes remaining before everyone was to leave. His was curious to see if he could identify Tyler as he came out of the building, although he had nothing to go by aside from age. He would then go in to speak with the therapist once everyone had left. He was prepared for a long sit and had brought his laptop with him to catch up on some work. Two of the men who eventually emerged could have been Tyler, but he had no way of knowing, as both were wearing long pants and neither was noticeably limping, which would have suggested a prosthesis. One of them was slightly taller and bearded. He wondered to himself why he thought he would recognize him.

Once the building was cleared, Adam grabbed one of his now infamous flyers and headed to the door. Walking up the broken concrete steps, he felt his heart race. Knocking on the big wooden door, which had been left ajar, Adam peered inside. The room was dark, except for a small amount of light from the small windows on one wall. The dark wooden floors were shiny with varnish. Six wooden chairs sat in a circle in the center of the room. This was as uninviting as anything Adam had ever seen, yet these patients came here out of a need to go somewhere for help.

A kindly looking man, short in stature, who looked to be in his sixties, greeted Adam. Stepping towards the man, Adam introduced himself to this rumpled-looking gent. The therapist introduced himself as Dr. Denison. He had eyes that were nearly wrinkled shut, a full, bushy beard and a generous girth. He wore a beige cardigan and brown corduroy pants. Dr. Denison was dressed like the quintessential group counsellor, which made Adam chuckle to himself. Adam had decided to go with his flyer theory after all but from a slightly different angle.

After showing Dr. Denison the flyer and explaining what he wanted in more detail than he had on the phone, Dr. Denison looked at him and asked, "So, why here specifically? Why this particular group, and why down here, south of the border?"

Adam swallowed the lump in his throat as he lied to the man, "It was random. I really couldn't find suitable groups where I practice. And being over the line, there's a greater chance of maintaining anonymity."

After a lengthy conversation and upon gaining the consent

of Dr. Denison, Adam arranged to attend a group therapy class in two weeks' time. Adam felt delirious with gratification. He stood up, very composed, appearing almost stoic for fear of exposing his feelings.

"Keep in mind, some of these guys have had very little social or emotional support. I have one young man here who woke from a coma only to find himself less a leg, living in a different state with nothing familiar, no friends, and a disconnected father. Mother has tried but seems at a loss. There was concern that he might try to self-harm, so these sessions have become important if we can keep him engaged."

Adam immediately knew Dr. Denison was talking about Tyler, so he told the therapist that this was one area where he really believed he could help. He assured the therapist that he was not here to outdo or override any treatment that was on-going - he only wanted to observe, as part of his research.

Fortunately, both doctors agreed that part of the job was to arrive at the best diagnosis when a complex set of symptoms is presented. More so than other mental health professionals, psychologists are experts in conducting psychological tests. But in Adam's case, the plan was to have him do nothing and not ask anything personal of Dr. Denison's patients.

"I have five men in this group, it just happened that way. One of them often doesn't show up, but I speak with his doctor from time to time. He's slightly antisocial and we won't want to discourage him, so we don't make a big deal about it when he shows up and we don't scold if he doesn't."

Adam had arrived, and now there was no turning back. If only he knew where Marin was. He arranged to be back for the assigned session, and in his mind, he planned to be there, regardless of what he had to cancel to make it happen.

* * * *

THE DAY ARRIVED, AND ADAM had walked into the building
on rubber legs. He was now sitting in on the first session. He
was finally in the same room as Tyler. He felt almost giddy
and imagined this was how Henry Morton Stanley felt when
he finally came face-to-face with Livingstone. While visibly
chipper, Adam worried that his expression would look too
happy, almost moronic, as this was not the place to be overly
gleeful. Trying hard to contain his enthusiasm, he had chosen
a seat away from the patients.

Adam positioned himself where he could study Tyler's
face without appearing as though he was staring at him. Tyler
looked nothing like Adam would have imagined him. He
was quite fair-haired, of average height, but his face was what
stood out. He was quite handsome, and there was a sorrowful
wisdom in his eyes. He wore a well-groomed beard. Tyler's
voice was unusually deep, seeming to come from someone
else, but his voice was soothing and calm. It was hard for
Adam to tell if his impression was based on his journey to find
this love of Marin's or if it was just a typical assessment of a guy
in a room.

A short, fit-looking man seemed anxious to speak. He was
almost scowling when he introduced himself as Carl. From
his remarks, Adam worked out that he had been in a boating
accident with his brother, Fred, who had been killed when the
vessel had flipped. Carl had tried many times to contact Fred's
wife afterwards, but she said there was no need for them to

see each other anymore. It was so final. He decided there was no point to anything. Fred was his only brother, and now he was estranged from his sister-in-law and his two nephews. He wanted to die. He spoke at length, and when he was finished, he simply stood up and left the room.

Adam's gaze turned to Tyler, who seemed reluctant to open up about what happened, but after seeing the nod from Dr. Denison, he began to speak, slowly, about a few basic details before his accident.

He didn't introduce himself but simply began speaking. "I was starting my career as an electrician. I had upgraded my math and physics in Washington, and I had taken level one of the apprenticeship program."

Dr. Denison interjected by saying, "We have a guest with us today, Tyler. He's here from Canada to see if he can help us out with some of our more immediate issues. Perhaps you'd like to jump ahead and share some of the reasons why you are here."

Tyler nodded and stared at his shoes while he spoke. "I was pretty decent at soccer, back then. My tryouts had all been good. I had been in Tucson with my girlfriend and had an opportunity to play with them. It was an amazing experience. A few months after, at the end of February, I got the call to come to the front office. I knew they were going to sign me. It was a two-and-a-half-hour drive to Portland, and my girlfriend, Marin, came with me. It was a quick trip. On the way home, we stopped in Bellevue and got a little hammered. Anyway, we crashed the car."

Tyler's disposition changed instantly as he took a drink of water before continuing, more severely, "I had a traumatic brain injury and I lost my left leg, just below the knee. The doctors told me I had been in a medically induced coma for almost three months. While I was in the coma, Dad decided to move. Why right then? I mean, who does that? When I woke up, not only did I have to deal with the news that we now live in fucking Buffalo and I lost my leg, but I also learned that my girlfriend had died in the crash. Do you know what that did to me? It was my fault. I had been poking her to make her laugh."

"We've been through this, Tyler. Survivor's guilt is not uncommon. It doesn't mean you should blame yourself," said Dr. Denison.

"Yes, I get it, and I know it takes time." Tyler rolled his eyes, then spoke as though reciting something he'd heard often. "The grieving delayed my recovery. My brain was slow to come around; it was something to do with hormones." He was then back in the present moment as he said, "I would go over the accident over and over, thinking of how it was my fault. I felt so guilty and wished I could go back to do it differently. Anyway, once I started to recover from my injuries, I was able to continue the apprenticeship program here. My dad said even if I became a pro soccer player, I should always have something to fall back on." He said the words with a genuine sorrow in his voice. Adam was acutely attentive and was hanging on to every word. "But I was having a hard time moving on. The doctors worried I would have a heart attack because I had something they called 'broken heart syndrome.' Meanwhile, I'm dealing with my leg. Now, I'm not sure if I'm angry or bitter."

Adam piped in, "I'm sure it might be a bit of both. But you seem to be getting around really well, Tyler." He worried that he would be reprimanded for speaking out, yet he wanted to make a connection somehow.

"Well, I've always loved sports. That's part of it that keeps me going. I won't let this injury beat me. My doctor said I had PTSD and that's why I need to come to these sessions. But I come mostly because of my dad. He makes me feel like an invalid and makes me think that I need him. I have to get out of that mindset. So, the sessions have helped in that way. Last November, I decided to get back to my physiotherapy. I'm riding my bike again, which took a while. Thanks to the War Amps, I now have a modified prosthesis and a Velcro loop that attaches to the pedal on my artificial foot, and I clip in on my good foot. It is taking time, but so far it's working great."

* * * *

DRIVING HOME THAT EVENING, ADAM was oblivious to his fatigue, to the hour, or the traffic. He didn't even notice the rain that pounded relentlessly down on the road in front of him, his wipers running on high. All he could think of was his meeting with Tyler. He had sat with Dr. Denison after the patients had left, sharing thoughts about the session. He felt a bit ashamed, like an imposter who didn't really belong in that very personal session with people who were hurting. But he was high on euphoria, his endorphins peaking. More than anything, he wanted to speak with Tyler alone.

33

ADAM SPENT A FEW HOURS IN THE MORNING CATCHING UP on client appointments and then he called it an early day telling Anya he would be at home if he was needed. His exhaustion was extreme as he arrived home and headed straight for the kitchen. He had started the habit of working at the kitchen island, spreading his papers out, eating there . . . basically living in one room. Somehow, it made him feel closer to Sofia, which he thought was odd. Plus, he caught the best afternoon sun there.

The ring of his phone was the first other sound in the room, so quietly had he been sitting there, immersed in his work. He was very surprised when he saw the name on the call display. It was Barbara Murphy. He answered with some hesitation.

"So, Tyler came home today and told me about a new doctor that had sat in on yesterday's session. A doctor, he said, from Canada. That wouldn't happen to be you, would it? I thought I'd asked you to stay away. Why are you doing this?"

"I think Tyler is a grown man and he should be able to make decisions for himself. Mrs. Murphy, I'd like to come and see you again. Or I could come to your house?"

"No!" was the emphatic reply. "I don't want to see you. I

want you to go away."

Adam sighed. "That's not going to happen, I'm sorry. Would you prefer if we talk on the phone?"

"No, it would be harder for me over the phone." She let out a sigh that spoke volumes. "Okay, before you do something that might harm us, I will agree to tell you why we are here and why we don't need any extra attention. But then you have to promise to go away."

* * * *

THREE DAYS LATER, HE WAS again sitting face-to-face with Tyler's mother, in Beatnik's Bistro.

"I'm not necessarily crazy about telling you such personal stuff, but after all, you are a doctor, and Tyler seems to like you."

"Why don't you just take a deep breath and, as they say, dive right in," Adam said with a smile.

"I don't know how things got so out of hand. First of all, I need to go way back. I knew Marin's dad, Geoffrey, in college. I more than knew him. We were sweethearts. We had dated for nearly a year, and though I thought it was casual, he would often discuss plans for our future. I usually brushed those conversations off, as we were both very young and trying to get an education. We weren't really serious. During that first summer, I took a job at a small bistro in town to help pay for some of my college courses."

"I know. School can get expensive, can't it?" said Adam, encouraging her.

She nodded her head and smiled awkwardly. Adam

thought this woman had forgotten how to smile a long time ago. "Well, it was there, at the bistro, that I met Keith. He was funny and sexy and was very—how should I say it—persistent. So, I went out with him. I didn't feel like I was doing anything wrong. Geoffrey and I were just dating; it's not like we were engaged or anything. Anyway, I was young and Keith was exciting, and he was so different from Geoff. He was what you'd call 'an experienced man.' He was seven years older than me. He had a nice car, money, and he had pursued me with a vengeance."

Adam concurred in an effort to alleviate some of her discomfort, "When we are young, we need to shop around, to feel free to explore our options. It's too soon to think about forever. At least, for most people it is."

Barbara nodded. "Well, yes, that's what I told myself at the time. For all the months I had dated Geoffrey we behaved like saints." Barbara turned red and kept her eyes down. "It took Keith only three dates to get my pants off. And I got pregnant in about five minutes. We married almost right away, wanting to spare my family the embarrassment of a pregnancy. Then we packed up the car and moved to Kirkland where he started his company. Of course, I hardly knew him. When I thought about it, shortly after we were married, it was more lust than anything. He never was a romantic or passionate man. He just always got what he wanted, one way or another. I further realized just what a possessive and jealous man Keith was. Anyway, end of story. I had made my bed, but I had a beautiful little boy to be grateful for."

Barbara placed her elbows on the table and pressed her hands to her cheeks. "Back then I hadn't realized he knew I had been seeing Geoffrey. I thought I had kept that from him, but I remember the day of our wedding. We went outside of the hall, and there was Geoffrey, parked in his car, watching us from across the street. I'll never forget the look of pain on his face. Keith demanded to know who he was, and I told him. 'So, that's the famous Geoffrey Jackson,' he had said."

The waitress brought them coffee and Barbara ordered a plate of fries before continuing, "My life went downhill from there. Shortly after, Keith moved us to Kirkland, and things were somewhat peaceful. Insipidly peaceful. We stayed out of each other's way a lot. My life didn't turn out anything like I expected. Keith and I didn't love each other. He spent a lot of time away from home. I was somewhat invisible to him. But he took to Tyler, as the boy grew older. Suddenly, he was his whole life."

The waitress returned to the table with the fries. Adam took this as a good sign that she planned on staying and talking for longer. She picked up a few fries but didn't eat them right away.

"Then about five years ago, unfortunately and quite by coincidence, Geoff and his family moved into our neighbourhood. Only then did Keith start accusing me of trapping him with being pregnant with someone else's child."

Adam felt at a loss for words. This poor woman was a wreck. Her voice was hollow, the desolation showing on her face.

"I thought he'd lost his mind. It was when Keith saw me having coffee with Geoffrey that things became worse. That was the day he blindsided me by saying he believed Tyler wasn't even his son – and that he surely belonged to Geoff. All these years, he had always wondered if Geoff was the father, knowing I had been seeing Geoffrey when we met. But he never said a word about it before. Suddenly now, he started saying that Tyler looks more like Geoff than like him. I really thought he'd lost his mind," she repeated.

Adam wondered where this story was going, but now it slowly started to make sense. He let the woman keep talking.

"Tyler was already seeing Marin, but this was before Keith knew Geoffrey was Marin's dad. Keith began acting strange after he caught us not just once, but a few times. Keith, in one of his jealous rages, confronted me, asking me if I had anything to do with Geoffrey moving here. Had I stayed in touch all these years."

"Is there any chance it could have been Geoffrey's baby? If I may ask you that?"

Barbara shook her head. "No, not possible. I was a virgin when I met Keith, and he knew it. Geoffrey and I dated, yes, and he had big dreams for our future. But he said we would wait until we got married to have sex. He was very old fashioned that way. But Keith was the opposite. I guess there was something exciting about it, when he forced himself on me. But it did get out of hand.

What made it worse was when he found out Tyler was seeing Marin. And that Marin was the daughter of Geoffrey. He didn't want Tyler to get involved with a girl who could be his half-sister. He said that Geoffrey was as disgusting as I was, allowing our children to be together."

"So, you say you had met Geoffrey a few times?"

"Yes, the first two times were quite by accident. The third was because I asked to see him again. But he was over me, and I don't blame him. Actually, he didn't deserve me. He deserved much better. His wife was young and pretty, and Marin was a lovely girl. Only later did I discover he had problems of his own."

Adam was curious. "What kinds of problems?"

"His wife, Angie, was a bit of a closet drunk. It became public knowledge over time. Whether it was recent or not wasn't important. And Marin was a bit wild when Tyler met her. Keith told me he ran into Angie in town one day, much later, and told her that her husband, Geoffrey, had fathered our son, Tyler. He then asked her if she really thought it was a good idea that Marin was sleeping with her half-brother. Perhaps she started drinking after that. But the jury was out over whether she killed herself or not."

Adam was surprised. "Is that what the rumour was? That she killed herself, or was that the result of a police investigation?"

"The police said the result was inconclusive. I have no idea if they are still working on it because we moved away. But it is quite a mystery. Was she pushed? Did she jump because of what Keith told her, or because she thought Marin would die from her injuries? Did she blame herself for letting Marin go with Tyler that day? Who knows?"

Without warning, Barbara changed her stance. She looked at Adam, almost sneering. "So, you haven't yet told me why you are here," Barbara snapped.

"Don't you think Tyler should know about Marin?"

She shook her head vehemently. "I can't tell him now. He'll hate me for keeping it from him. I think he'll get over it; he's still young."

"But do you agree with your husband? Do you think Tyler and Marin should be kept apart? After all, you know they aren't related. And you said yourself how unhappy he is. Surely, there must be more to life for him. At least, he should have the option. They both should, if for no other reason than closure. They deserve to be able to say goodbye to one another."

"Well, life is just a series of disappointments, isn't it? They might as well learn that now," was Barbara's stoic response.

"So, Keith is prepared to ruin his son's life because of his own agenda and based on his unfounded suspicions. Do as I say, not as I do, is that it?"

"Yes, but isn't that what parents do?" answered Barbara with an almost frightening sincerity. "Life is no picnic; I've already learned that. I mean, look at me. I'm forty-four years old and I look sixty."

Adam wanted badly to disagree with her, but she was right.

"Shouldn't that be his choice and not yours or your husband's? Besides, he'll hate you more if he finds out in another fifteen or twenty years. Do you want him to feel sixty when he's forty-four?"

Barbara looked down and appeared on the verge of tears.

Adam berated himself for saying that, and for it coming out so harshly. He softened his tone before continuing, "But Mrs. Murphy, you now have an opportunity to see that your son doesn't waste the possibilities that he could have. Wouldn't you want him to not make the mistake you made? What if he lost this one chance? Would you regret it forever? Would he forgive you?" Adam then thought, to himself, *because I will tell him, one way or another.* "Mrs. Murphy, is your husband involved with a man called Jose-Luis? I need to tell you something now. If you know of someone by that name, you might want to tell your husband that this man is under arrest and he will likely go to jail. There are people lined up to testify against him, and I'm afraid the police will want your husband to make a statement as well."

Barbara Murphy grabbed her bag and moved to the edge of

her chair, ready to take flight.

Adam was going to lose her. He needed to speak quickly. "They know where you are, and they will be in contact. You don't have to let on you know about it. I don't know what this man meant to you, but I know your husband knew him. Is this why you think I am here?"

Barbara Murphy was already standing up, and with nothing more than a goodbye, walked out the door. But today she was visibly crying. The woman was a master at avoidance. Frustrated, Adam flung his napkin onto the table.

* * * *

ADAM FELT OVERWHELMED BY THE events of the past few weeks and wanted some time away from his thoughts. For him, the best thing right now was this distraction. He had a glass of wine on the table beside him, and he was once again working on Sofia's dresser. The hard work of stripping was nearly finished. He was currently working on the fine sanding, removing the residue with a damp cloth, gently running his hand over the wood, checking for smoothness. His angst now subsiding, Adam caressed the wood lovingly, checking carefully for imperfections. He wanted it to be perfect. He was certain she would be pleased at the way it had turned out, and in his head, he imagined her delicate laughter. Tomorrow, he would apply the stain.

Whether this was cognitive avoidance or substitutive avoidance, it seemed to be working, as all thoughts of the Murphys and the Jacksons had temporarily vanished.

34

ADAM SAT LOOKING AT TYLER. THIS WAS THE SECOND TIME
they had sat together. The group session had ended, and Dr.
Denison was outdoors speaking with Carl. Adam and Tyler
were the only two sitting in the room. Tyler didn't seem in a
hurry and had eased into a conversation with Adam. Today,
Adam knew he had connected with Tyler in the way he had
hoped. He also knew he couldn't keep this up. He could possibly get away with one more session before Keith or Barbara
Murphy came barrelling down on the group and possibly
withdrawing Tyler or, worse, exposing Adam.

"So, knowing I'd be tied down for some time, with school
and sports, Marin and I decided to drive to Tucson to ride in
the El Tour race, just for fun. We weren't worried about our
time, and so took one of the shorter routes. We stayed out of
the way of the real riders. It's actually a pretty singular event.
It was just a final fling holiday. While we were there, we went
on a hike the next day with some of the riders. They took us to
Oro Valley, to the Catalina State Park, where we hiked up to
this amazing place called Romero Pools. We both loved it and
swore we'd come back.

Then at the end of February, the Portland Timbers had

invited me to Casa Grande, Arizona, to come and kick the ball around with them. It was during their training camp. We flew down, as it had to be a really short trip. While we were there, we attended a game. Tucson had won the best regular-season record in the Western Conference, so they hosted the conference final four at Kino North Stadium. They defeated the Vancouver Whitecaps in the Under 23 Division, which was great because they are Portland's rivals. They beat them in the conference semifinals. It was a special trip for Marin and me.

"We hiked back to that place, Romero Pools, in the Catalina Mountains, and I asked her to marry me."

"I've been there," Adam said.

"You've been where? To Romero Pools?" Tyler sat up in is chair.

"Well, I didn't quite make it, I fell off a small cliff and hurt myself. But I was up there, and I was very near the pools."

"Well, it became a special place for us. I'd like to go back there some day."

Adam remained silent, remembering Claire's words. Was it too soon to tell Tyler about Marin? Did he think Tyler was ready to hear the words?

"My dad hit the roof when he heard we got engaged. He went on this rant about how I didn't know what I was doing and I wasn't capable, nor was Marin. Christ, he was treating us like *Benny and Joon*, like we couldn't handle life. Man, life got tense after that." Tyler stood up and stretched. "Can we walk?"

"Sure, that sounds like a good idea," said Adam, also standing.

Once outside, the cold hit Adam and he cursed under his breath as he tucked his hands deep into his pockets. He caught

Dr. Denison's disapproving glare from the corner of his eye but ignored him. The street was noisy with the sound of traffic and honking horns. The smell of exhaust was nauseating, adding to Adam's discomfort.

None of this seemed to bother Tyler, who had started talking again. "I still have nightmares. Look at me. I'm pathetic. My dad loves having this control over my life. He owns me. My leash is short, and he doesn't let me go too far. Here I am, a twenty-four-year-old cripple living at home. In fucking Buffalo, of all places. I have PTSD and most mornings I wake up and I can't breathe. I don't want any of their drugs. There's nothing great about any of this. I want my life back. I want Marin back."

"You really loved her, didn't you?"

"Love her. Present tense, please. Yes, I love her madly. I knew it by the third conversation I had with her. That was my turning point. The day I knew my life had changed forever. I wanted to take care of her. Protect her and encourage her. I wanted to watch her grow, and I wanted to grow along with her. We both lacked the confidence. Well, she lacked it more than me, especially after my father's reaction. So I think I was definitely more confident than she was, but wow, she was amazing, and smart. Well, I didn't do such a good job of protecting her, did I?"

Adam turned to Tyler and said, "So, why do you stay? I mean, you're good-looking, bright, and you have a good trade. You could get out of here. Move."

Tyler laughed. "Yeah, right. And go where?

"I don't know, maybe back home to Washington? You just said you hate Buffalo."

"I don't have a home anymore. Marin was my home, so what's the point? I have money but nothing to spend it on. I earn it and stash away. Doesn't matter where I am, I don't care anyway. I lost my heart. Do you have any idea what that feels like? It's worse than losing a leg, I'll tell you. It's like, I eat because I'm hungry and because I need to eat. All I can think of is that I killed the only person I'll ever love. It's been years, but I don't love her any less. I think it's because I've had no closure you know?"

"Tyler, above all else you have to feel good about yourself. Then other things will happen because you will start to allow them to happen. It won't work the other way around."

"Yes, I know. They talk a lot of Jung to me. I can't change anything until I accept it. But it should have been me that died, not her. I just wish I could say sorry. Sorry that I hurt her. It was my fault." After a few minutes, Tyler added, "I write to her, you know."

"To Marin?"

He nodded. "Yeah. I write her a letter about once a month. It's always helped me, and it's way better than any of these sessions."

"What do you say to her?"

"I tell her how much I miss her. I let her know how I'm doing. I want to know what happened to her. Did she die instantly? Did she suffer?"

They walked in silence for a few minutes. Adam got it. The bit about only having one love. Sofia was the first time he had felt love, and he couldn't even comprehend loving anyone else. And whether she stayed or not, he would love only her. He had no way to tell if anyone else would eventually come along to fill his days, but it didn't mean that Sofia wouldn't forever be his one and only love. The heart was big enough to love again, but not all in the same way.

Tyler looked angry. "My mom is miserable, and my dad is an asshole. I don't know why they are married. My dad never treated my mom with the respect she deserved. They do it wrong, and then try to tell me how to do it right. So, marrying the wrong person for the wrong reason is supposed to be okay? Yet, I wanted to marry Marin. She might have been the wrong person in my dad's eye, but it was for the right reason. That should mean something. What I mean is, we had our lives mapped out. What right did he have to take that away from us? Maybe he's assuming I'd be like him? He robbed us. I hate him."

Adam felt he should say something, but he also thought it was good to let Tyler vent. He hadn't spoken this much in the time he had known him.

Tyler kicked at a chunk of snow that had begun to melt itself free from a pile. "I can still remember how she smells." His words were more to himself than to Adam. Then he said to Adam, "I know I let my dad down. He loved that I played soccer. It was a hard pill for us both to swallow, losing soccer as my career."

"But nobody should be alone." Adam's words sounded flimsy, but he was struggling for better ones. The guilt at not saying anything was weighing on him, heavily.

"I'm not alone. Marin's with me, and I don't want that to sound creepy because it isn't. It's not been long enough for me to want to move on. Besides, love is not the same for everyone. There's no universal feeling that we all go through;

it's so individual for each of us. I don't think I want anyone to understand what it's like for me. It's private. It's mine, and it's something nobody can take away from me."

* * * *

Driving home, Adam went over and over his conversation with Tyler. Lying in bed that night, he looked at Sofia's robe hanging on the back of the door. He pictured her taking it off and hanging it on the hook, then walking naked to the bed to climb in beside him. He missed her so much that it ached. Reaching for his phone, he looked at the clock. It would be crazy to call now. He would have to wait until morning. But he needed to talk to her. It was time for her to come home. The night brought little sleep, and by five, he could wait no longer.

"Adam. Is everything okay?"

"Yes, I'm fine, Sofia. I just need you to come home. You should be here with me." Adam was referring to the latest tragedy on the news. A few weeks ago, a woman only a bit older than Sofia had been found murdered in her Florence apartment. She was an American woman, who had been strangled by an illegal immigrant from Senegal. "You are not safe there, on your own."

Sofia sounded calm. "But, Adam, I'm not in Florence. I'm safely at home with my family. Plus, you are forgetting that I am Italian. I don't stand out. Please don't worry; I live a quiet life here. That American woman, she lived a different life, and she lived it in Florence. The circumstances were very different. Adam, I will be home soon, I promise."

Adam spoke in quiet tones, and Sofia picked up on the

unusual silence. "Okay, maybe that's not the real reason I want you home. I feel your absence and I miss us."

"Your voice sounds funny. What's wrong?" Sofia said, concern in her voice.

"It's still the thing with this guy, Tyler. I have made some progress and have connected with him. But I am getting a lot of opposition from people about my tactics. I'm just trying to help him reconnect with someone who meant very much to him. Is that so wrong?"

Sofia's voice soothed him instantly. "It's not a bad thing, my love. If it helps you to sleep at night, do it. Can you picture his future, and yours, if you do nothing?"

And right there, Adam had his answer.

35

Marin rested comfortably on her journey home to Tucson. Fortunate to have been assigned a window seat, she sat enjoying the sun on her face. To say her trip home was bizarre would be putting it mildly. She discovered things that she found to be categorically unfathomable. Yet, the effect it had on her was that of a calm deliverance of sort from so many things that had plagued her. She just wished she had known these things sooner. One thing Marin knew for certain was that she would never return to Washington. She didn't need any reminders of that pitiful, broken life.

It was a short walk through the arrivals gate to the exits. Marin practically ran down the escalator and out into the sunshine. Penelope was waiting outside, her car stood running at the curb. Marin quickly threw her bag into the open trunk and jumped into the car. The security man was heading towards them - no doubt to tell Penelope that she was in a "no parking" zone. Marin gave the man a wave and a smile, and climbed into the car. Within seconds, they were on their way. Marin looked over at her smiling friend.

"You look like the Cheshire Cat. What are you smiling at?" questioned Marin.

"I guess you haven't read the papers lately, have you?" was Penelope's opening remark.

Marin shook her head in confusion.

"Your story—the one you wrote about the bears in Green Valley? It won the story of the month prize, or something like that. They ran it again a few days ago."

"No way!" shouted Marin.

"Haven't you been checking your emails?"

"Not on my work phone. I left that turned off and in my bag. This wasn't a working holiday, so they told me not to have it on. They said I had enough to deal with." Marin wanted to scream loud and long, just for the release. "Take me for something to eat, Penny. I'll tell you a story you won't believe."

By the time Penelope had finished her dinner, Marin had finished the retelling of her trip home. Penny was sitting staring at her friend, seeming incapable of saying anything. She was looking at Marin with a "what now?" expression.

Marin then said, "It's funny, you know? I had a bad accident, after which I packed up and left Washington once I was able to. I had this notion that by coming to Tucson all my troubles would be over. I could never figure out why that didn't happen. I was plagued by my memories. But going back helped, it really did. I have a better sense of what happened, although I'll never know why a lot of it happened. I have no plans of going back to that place, even though I love my dad and my sister. I will see them from time to time, but they will need to come here. I like who I am, Penny. And I love my Arizona life. It's as simple as that, with or without Tyler."

Try as she might, there would be no sleeping for Marin. She knew she would need to do a lot of napping over the weekend to be ready for work on Monday. Also at the back of her mind was the woman at the office of El Tour de Tucson. She concluded there would be no point in calling, because once again, she had neglected to get the name of the person she was dealing with. It would be next to impossible to find the woman she was speaking with—the proverbial needle in a haystack situation. March was half over, and Marin found it hard to believe this much time had passed. It was definitely too late to expect to hear anything.

* * * *

THE WEEKEND FLEW BY, AND Marin was again at work, where she was greeted with a barrage of congratulatory whistles and pats on the back. Her boss smiled approvingly and gave her a thumbs-up. Her slated promotion was intact. Marin had texted Jay to invite him and George for dinner. She wasn't sure how much she would tell them, aside from the fact that her family was well. Totally screwed up, but well. But all Marin wanted to do was see her friends again.

The three had arranged to meet at a little restaurant half way between them, at Oracle and Magee Roads. This restaurant had the best outdoor dining patio. It was quite private, with ample shade provided by the vine-covered pergola, and had lots of colour, courtesy of the bright tablecloths and an abundance of hanging baskets brimming with flowers. A massive bamboo partition provided seclusion and a bit of a sound barrier from the street. The cobbled floor was reminiscent of Mexico or Europe. The music was soft and eclectic. Once settled, lots of hugs later, Jay's first expression was to congratulate Marin for her award.

"It was a good story."

"I'm surprised, as I was in agony over missing my dinner with Adam. Maybe that will be my secret to success. Stress journalism."

"And what about your mystery man? Any word?" George was in between mouthfuls of arancini and calamari, two of his favourite antipasti dishes.

Marin shook her head and reflected, "Adam will have to remain a sweet memory. I suppose I had no real reason to find him, other than to say goodbye and to ask if he was okay. But who knows, maybe I'll see him this year in November, at El Tour. Could it happen that I would run into him twice?" She looked at George and humbly asked, "Can I ask for more than one milagro without seeming greedy?"

Jay sat up and said to Marin, "We haven't told you yet. The Mission was vandalized again."

"Vandalized how?" This was terrible news, and Marin was visibly upset.

"Graffiti everywhere. Someone spray painted six-six-six and 'Hail Satan' and other satanic things. They sprayed all across the front and down the sides of the Mission. The building already has been undergoing renovations for the past few years, and now this setback. Black spray paint everywhere. It will cost money to remove and then to re-plaster and white-wash. People in the community and everywhere are outraged. The are not eager to go another round of fundraising, already feeling the fatigue of what they call begging."

The enjoyable visit came to a close, and Marin had lingered saying goodbye to her friends. Now weary, she lay in bed, having decided against the bath. She had had enough thinking for the time being. Also, Marin had just read a text message from her roommate, Stella. One more complication was heading her way.

* * * *

MARIN'S LIFE BECAME A BIT of a whirlwind for the following weeks. It was almost in desperation that she was trying to regain normalcy, get her life back on track. She bounced back and forth from work to socializing with a new intensity, almost frenzy.

Right now, Penelope and Marin were sitting inside a brightly lit, noisy bistro, enjoying their Buddah bowls. The spicy aromas filled the room, kicking Marin's senses into high gear. Penelope had finally agreed to see a movie, and they had left early in an ambitious attempt to fit in lunch prior to heading over to the theatre.

Marin, who had been bringing her friend up to speed with the week's activities, suddenly blurted out, "To top it off, I got a long message from Stella. She's coming home, and she's bringing her boyfriend. I mean, it is her place and all, but it sounds like they will be here together for at least a month." Marin moaned and placed her hands over her face in mock agony. "I think it might be time for me to get my own place."

Penelope was scrutinizing her, her eyes seemed to be taking every inch of Marin's face. She didn't appear to be listening.

"What?" said Marin, shielding her face from the stares of her friend.

"You've got great hair. You should wear it down more often."

I'll stop.

Marin relaxed and laughed. Point made. She needed to loosen up and stop worrying.

"Bob says yoga helps," Penelope responded as Marin exhaled.

"So, who is Bob?"

Penelope grinned ear to ear. "Didn't I tell you? Bob's my new boyfriend."

"You're going out with a guy named Bob?"

"I'll tell you about him in the theatre. Come on, we're going to be late, and this is your movie."

* * * *

IT WAS TUESDAY, AROUND MIDDAY when Marin's phone rang. Looking at the call display, she didn't recognize the number but answered nonetheless. In her line of work, she often received calls from people she didn't know.

"Good day, Ms. Jackson, I don't know if you remember me." Marin immediately recognized the voice. It was the woman from El Tour. "Sorry to bother you, but I am going through our registrations for this years' ride, and I have this application on my screen that made me think of you. I might have your fellow—the one from Toronto. Now, I can't guarantee anything, but the best I can offer is, if you write a note—which I will need to read for content mind you—I can pass it forward to the address I have on file, and that's the best I can do."

"Yes, oh yes, please," Marin responded with a frenzied excitement. The woman gave Marin an email address where she was to send her note. As she was typing, she suddenly felt foolish and didn't quite know what to say, just that she hoped he was feeling better and wouldn't be frightened away from coming back after his fall. She reminded Adam that she would hike to Romero Pools on April 12 and she would think of him, as she understands it's unlikely he would come. Maybe he would return next November, and she could hike with him then. She signed it, "Your friend, Marin," leaving her email address.

That night, Marin lay in bed, watching the ceiling fan go round and round, hypnotizing her but not enough to make her sleepy. It was the first warm evening after a hot day. Spring had arrived with temperatures having reached ninety. Her life was about to change again. Stella was coming home. Normally, Marin would have been excited at the prospect of having another body in the house again—someone to share things with and all—but she was less thrilled about the curveball Stella had thrown her by announcing she wouldn't be coming alone. Tomorrow, Marin would start looking for places. It would be easier for her to afford something on her own with her pending raise. Her promotion would be announced in June, she was told.

But biggest on her mind were recent events—revelations of family, the new possibility of finding Adam, but mostly Tyler's approaching birthday. She was beginning to say her goodbyes to him forever. Marin felt torn up inside. Why did she ever believe that he was out there somewhere? Maybe she never did. He had just felt so alive inside her. After all, if he was in fact alive, surely, he would have come looking for her. She tried not to think of that.

36

As the meeting drew to a close, Adam had already decided he wasn't coming back. As the participants stood and had begun their departures, Adam hurriedly followed Tyler outside to speak to him alone. He didn't look back to see if Dr. Denison was watching him, knowing the man had been waiting for the session to end so that he might have a word. Dr. Denison was clearly not impressed with Adam's behaviour.

Catching up with Tyler, Adam began speaking in a cool and easy manner. "I realize it's not acceptable to discuss issues outside of the sessions, but do you want to go grab a beer? We could talk about Arizona and cycling. Or Romero Pools. I'd like to talk about Romero Pools, if that's okay. I'd like to tell you about someone who went through exactly what you did," said Adam.

Tyler quickly said yes. "I think I need a real conversation, not a patronizing bunch of shit."

Adam knew the time had come to give up the charade. There wasn't a chance in hell he was going to continue lying to Tyler, knowing what he knew. He remained silent as Tyler directed him around the corner to a bar and grill. Stepping inside, Adam was surprised to see it so lively at this time of day. I guess there was little else to do around here in the winter. They seated themselves at a table by the window.

"Tyler, I need to ask you something. If you knew Marin was alive somewhere and was unhappy without you, where would you be right now?" Adam didn't want to waste any time getting to the point.

"If I thought it was true, I'd feel braver about getting out of here, away from my dad. But we know it's too late for that. Maybe this is my destiny."

"Tyler, I need you to listen to me for a minute." He pulled his chair up closer. "I have to tell you something that I wanted to tell you sooner."

"Um, okay," Tyler said, turning slightly to face him. He began casually rubbing his fingers along the surface of the creviced wooden table.

Taking a deep breath, he looked at Tyler and said, "What if I told you Marin was alive, and I know where she is?"

Tyler froze, his face lost all colour and was contorting in disbelief. He stopped breathing, and his hands tensed into fists. Then slowly, the colour returned to his face and his breath came back in gasps. "What do you mean she's alive? How do you know? Is this a sick joke?"

"No, it's true. I met her when I was hiking to Romero Pools. When I fell, she was the one who helped me down the mountain. She was the one who told me about you. It's the only reason I'm here, Tyler. To find you." Adam stopped talking and sat back, wanting to give Tyler room to digest this information.

Tyler sat still, looking from Adam to the floor and back. He scratched his beard, trying to make some sense of this news.

Adam tried hard not to stare at Tyler. He gazed elsewhere to give Tyler some privacy—as much as was possible when seated across from each other. Adam was well aware as to how overwhelming this was for Tyler to process. Once or twice, Tyler opened his mouth as if to speak but fell silent again. He sat looking around the room, then back at Adam, shaking his head and sighing. After a few minutes, Adam spoke again. "Your dad has been lying to you, Tyler."

"But why didn't you tell me right away?" Tyler's disbelief was slowly morphing into anger.

"I was hoping your mom would have talked to you."

"My mom knows my dad was lying? What the hell is going on? Why would they do that? And how do you know?"

"You'll have to talk to your mom. Or your dad."

"Okay, so you're supposed to be my friend. When did you talk to my mom? Why did you wait so long to tell me?" Tyler's anger had now turned to grief, and his eyes were welling up.

"I'm a doctor. My first concern was for your state of mind. Then I wanted to be sure you felt the same way as Marin."

"And what way is that?"

"Lonely. Guilty. In love with you."

"And you say she's alive and in Arizona? Right now?"

"Yes, she is. And here is where you have the chance to change your life. You can go to her, start over, if that's what you both decide to do. But I think you need to talk to your mom, and probably your dad as well, so you can understand what is going on."

"Do you know what's going on?" Tyler asked abruptly.

Adam shook his head. "Not entirely. I only know parts of it. I haven't spoken to your dad, although I would have liked to. But I doubt he would have wanted to speak to me. I heard something about a man named Jose-Luis that your dad—and maybe Marin's dad as well—may have been mixed up with. Apparently, this guy is one bad dude, works for a Mexican cartel. But it doesn't make sense to me. Why would your dad suddenly pull up roots and leave everything behind? Why would he be here in Buffalo, starting a new life, breaking all ties to Washington, purely because of Marin? So, you see, Tyler, none of this is really any of my business."

"And yet here you are." said Tyler, adding, "I don't mean to sound disrespectful."

Adam sighed. "Yes, and yet here I am. I'm here for Marin. Actually, Marin doesn't even know I'm here." Adam paused and then continued, "Okay, I guess I'm here for me. But mostly for you and Marin."

Tyler sat forward, leaning his elbows on his knees. "Okay, so what did my mom say to you?"

"Well, this is the hard part for me, but I think you should have a conversation with them. But regardless of what they say, you don't have to listen to them. The final decision is yours. I just think you should talk to them. I know you are scared, and I don't feel great about being an instigator. But you are not sixteen; you are an adult. You don't need to be afraid of your father."

"But you have seen what he is capable of."

Adam sat forward, wanting to catch Tyler's eyes. "But what are *you* capable of, Tyler? Okay, let's talk about destiny then, shall we? You need to move forward in life, not stagnate. That means you need to be open to possibilities and I know that gives you anxiety. But if you give up on that anxiety, you will

Alyssa Hall

stay depressed. What is a life without possibilities? Without fulfilling our dreams? So, you have a choice here—stagnation or freedom? Marin's out there, Tyler. You have to work hard for the happy ending. Accept the anxiety. The good part won't just fall into your lap. Tyler, I won't be back. Here's my card if you want to talk to me. I know the good Dr. Denison will want this for you. I'll let him know I won't be back."

An ashen Tyler looked distraught, the tears continuing to well in the corners of his eyes. "I have an appreciation of life that I never had before. It took years for me to get my head on right. I just don't know where to go from here," said Tyler.

"You should know that Marin said almost the exact same thing, Tyler," uttered Adam in amazement.

"But I don't get it. If she's alive, why hasn't she tried to find me?" Then he looked at Adam with a flash of realization. "She wouldn't have been able to find me, would she?"

"Marin was told that you died. She doesn't know you are alive."

Tyler shook his head and, in a hushed voice, continued. "I have to go home. I have to talk to my dad. I feel sick, knowing how my life has been manipulated." Tyler got up fast and, in doing so, knocked his chair over. He turned around and aimed to kick it again, but instead, stood it carefully on its legs. He then stormed out of the room. Adam sat, menu still in hand.

* * * *

THAT EVENING, ADAM CALLED CLAIRE, asking her if he could speak with her. She was in the neighbourhood and said she could be there in ten minutes. Adam hung up the phone and

- 226 -

began pacing. Claire arrived in five, and Adam poured them each a glass of wine. The two of them went into the living room and Adam put the fire on before sitting down opposite Claire.

After listening to Adam, Claire quietly said, "This is tragic. As I said before, it's almost like *Romeo and Juliet*. Here we have two feuding families, and it's the kids who suffer. Each thinks the other is dead, and neither are looking forward to a life without the other."

Adam looked at Claire. "Seriously? Is that the analogy you want to make? *Romeo and Juliet*? Let's hope that Marin and Tyler don't get the same stupid idea. These two are fragile enough as it is."

"I meant the love part, silly. That and the fact that their families are trying to keep them apart. But, Adam, this is compelling stuff. It's like you've broken the curse because now Tyler knows. He's on to them."

"Yes, and the rest is now up to him," Adam said as he swallowed his wine in one gulp.

Claire stood up, and as she turned to leave the room, Adam called to her.

"Can I ask you something personal?"

"Anything," she said, turning to face him. "You know you can ask me anything."

"Do you ever wish you had children of your own? I mean, do you regret your decision to not have any?"

Claire took a lingering step forward then stopped. Her eyes softened as she answered him. "My life became very different after I met your father. I mean, after Will, when I really started to know your father and you. I found a peace and normalcy with the two of you, unlike anything I had ever known. So, I might have regretted it, if it wasn't for you, Adam. You brought me such joy. Such fulfillment. Being there and watching you grow up, sharing moments like your first puppy, or when you learned to ride a bike."

"But my puppy died, and I had a bad accident on my bike."

Claire laughed. Now I see where this is going. I can't tell you what to do, but I can tell you how I think Sofia feels. Don't be so afraid. You will never be able to protect your kids from little things like that - the lessons of life. But you can teach them better ways to deal with these things and with bigger things. You can teach love and trust and consequences, and honour and honesty. That's all you can do, Adam. There are no guarantees. And if you ask me, I think you would be a terrific father, and unlike me, you would regret not having children."

Adam sat and smiled as he watched Claire leave.

37

Tyler walked into the house. He closed the door behind him quietly, listening for the sound of his father. Hearing the sound of the television, he made his way to the front room. There he found his dad, reading the paper. His mother sat nearby in an easy chair, apparently asleep. Her head was resting against the back of the chair, and her mouth was partly open. Tyler approached without a word and sat in the chair furthest away from his father. He looked at his dad with pure contempt.

"Dad? Mom? Can I talk to you guys?" Without waiting for an answer, Tyler cleared his throat and began. "So, Dad, it seems Marin is alive. But I didn't have to tell you that, did I?" He was prepared to be emphatic in a way he had never been before.

Keith sat up, caught off guard by his son's remarks. But he didn't flinch. "No, you didn't have to tell me. But I had to tell you! That girl's done you enough harm. What good is it knowing she's still around?"

"The accident was my fault, Dad. Not hers. You had no right to lie to me," shouted Tyler.

Keith clenched his fists. "Well, it was too late; the damage was done. I don't give a rat's ass anymore whose fault it was. There's no going back. It was the right decision to tell you she was dead."

Tyler didn't back down. "It was the wrong decision." He turned his head. "You too, Mom. What is going on here?"

His mom sat up and spoke softly, parroting her husband's sentiments. "There's no point going back."

"Isn't there?" Tyler spoke directly to her. "If you're driving home and you realize you've taken a wrong turn, do you keep going? NO! You turn around, don't you? Because you don't know where you will end up if you carry on down that road!"

Keith was standing now, and he fired back at his son. "It was too late, I tell you. Goddammit, Tyler. It was too late because it wasn't because of Marin, okay? It was because of someone else."

"Okay, so was it because of someone named Jose or whatever?" questioned Tyler.

Keith looked at his son and held his breath. "How do you know about him?"

"The same way I found out that Marin is alive."

"It's that doctor, isn't it?" asked Barbara.

"What doctor?" It was Keith's turn to look confused.

Barbara looked down. She had no intention of mentioning her conversation with Adam. "The one who gave you the flyer on the doorstep last month, I guess. He left his card on the doorstep; I picked it up the next morning."

"Just tell me what's going on, you two. Why don't I know? This is my life, too, that we are talking about. Stop being so disgusting, the pair of you."

Feeling defeated, his parents looked at one another, and

his dad sat down again. Together, Tyler's parents attempted to explain, starting at the beginning, with Barbara and Geoffrey and the ensuing fiasco surrounding her pregnancy. His mother assured Tyler none of it was true, and Keith admitted he'd been an ass.

Barbara got up and left the room so Keith and Tyler could have more privacy for this part of the conversation. Tyler watched his mother shuffle out of the room, and he no longer knew what he felt for her. Keith then began his explanation and the reason why he told his son Marin was dead.

"There's someone who is after me. It's a man who works for the cartel. A man named Jose-Luis. He tried to involve me in money laundering, but I kept saying no. Mine was not the kind of business where you could do that without drawing attention. The cartel was not taking no for an answer. They expected me to take over where the dead guy had left off, or they'd have to eliminate me as well. They couldn't have anyone out there talking because I knew too much."

Tyler sat back and crossed his arms. So far, he was hearing nothing that could convince him that lying was necessary.

"The man who died, Jimmy, had tried to get out of dealings with Jose-Luis, but he wouldn't let him quit, so he killed him." Keith explained to Tyler how bad it had become for this poor man, just by trying to walk away. "Jimmy had never wanted to cooperate in the first place, but he hung with the wrong guys and had unwittingly become involved."

Tyler sighed. "I'm still not getting it, Dad."

Keith looked at his son with an expression of humiliation. "I'm not saying he wasn't lured in at the thought of money, but he got scared. He'd come to me, gave me some books he wanted me to hold on to for him. Said he was getting out and he wanted to keep these away from Jose-Luis and the police. I told him no. Said I didn't want to get involved. I told him to take the books and shove it. I have no idea what was in them. I'll never forget the look on his face as he was leaving my office. I didn't know he'd be dead the next day."

Keith told Tyler he was not there at the time of the murder. He only went to play cards and smoke cigars and occasionally to drink scotch. He had no idea he was being recruited.

"Jose-Luis came to me a few days later and asked me for the books. I told him I didn't have them. He called me a liar. He said I would need to come clean, turn them over, and do as I was told. But you see, I knew he killed Jimmy. We all knew. We were all afraid to say anything. So, we left."

"But this is your deal, Dad. Not mine. Why the lie about Marin?" asked Tyler.

Keith was shouting at this point. "How did I know they didn't cause your accident? I thought they were sending me a warning, not to refuse them. When we left, I wanted to get away from the whole situation. Your mom and I had a narrow window of opportunity to come here. We told everyone we were going to Chicago. I didn't know if they would come looking for me. Then when we heard that Marin's mom was killed, we were afraid I might be next. I knew too much about the man, and the cartel would be furious that I ran and refused to work with them. They would cut off my fingers or my hands. Or worse, your hands or mom's hands." Keith's anger abated. "So, we came to Buffalo."

"Whoa, back up, Dad. Marin's mom is dead? What happened to her?" Tyler grabbed his head like it would explode.

Keith threw his hands up in frustration. "I don't know who killed her. I heard it might have been Jose-Luis. She had been snooping around, trying to find out what was going on. She thought her husband was also involved. I heard she confronted Jose-Luis and threatened to go to the police."

"So, get to the Marin part, Dad," said Tyler, his impatience growing.

"If you went back for her, they might have grabbed you or found out where we were."

"But why did Marin think I was dead?"

"Your mom told Geoffrey, so that he would spread the word."

"My life has become a lie. It's like I've been living in a Potemkin village. What else don't I know?"

"Listen Tyler, if you thought Marin was alive, you'd want to go back to Washington and I couldn't let that happen. I don't know what they'd have done to you."

"Dad, I don't believe you and I never will. We could have asked Marin to come here! You never liked her. You just wanted to move on, you and your happy little family, no matter the cost to me or mom."

"Listen to me, dammit. I obstructed justice. I could go to jail."

"So, why did you make that my business, too? Maybe you should go to jail. Isn't it a crime to fake someone's death?" There was anger in Tyler's tears. "Besides, there's more to the Jose-Luis story, isn't there, Dad?"

"What do you mean?" Keith went very quiet.

"I mean it all sounds too simple, Dad. He'd want to kill you because you said no? Did you keep the books? Or did you help this man with drugs? There must be more. Look at you, you are scared shitless."

Keith stood up and left the room without saying another word. He walked outside and slammed the door behind him.

38

As difficult as it was, Adam knew he needed to leave Tyler alone. Adam had dropped a bomb on him, with the revelation of Marin being alive, and of his father's involvement with the cover-up. It was now up to Tyler what his next move would be. It had been an exhausting couple of weeks, and Adam was sick of the trips to Buffalo. He was relieved that he wouldn't have to go back there. He also hoped he didn't in some way further damage Tyler's outlook on life. But still, Adam was certain that he was doing the right thing. Marin and Tyler were imperfect and vulnerable, but they were also in love, and Adam wanted so badly for them to succeed in their hopes and dreams.

The telephone conversation with Dr. Denison was easier than Adam had imagined, although the doctor was extremely annoyed at Adam's methods. It would have been easier, said Dr. Denison, if he had simply explained what he was up to. It actually would have been easier to stop playing cat and mouse and be upfront, or call local authorities, or knock on the Murphy door. Nonetheless, Dr. Denison said he would speak at length with Tyler. Adam didn't bother trying to explain the entire story: the threats on life, Jose-Luis, and a couple of suspicious deaths. He was just glad it was all over.

After finishing his shave, Adam stood gazing into the bathroom mirror. He wasn't looking at his unruly dark hair, very much in need of a trim. He wasn't looking at his eyes, intense and brooding under thick brows. Nor was he looking at his chiselled nose, straight and perhaps a bit too long. He was studying his expression, somber and heartsick. Although behind that, he saw something else, something that was telling him he was ready. He had been so afraid to have kids. It was time to stop remembering how he had felt when he was old enough to realize his mother was not around. Then it dawned on him that this was exactly the reason why he should have them. It would be healing for him. He would have the opportunity to do things differently. Kids can turn out okay despite the mistakes parents make. There will always be mistakes. No one is perfect. But with love and support, a person can thrive. Oddly, Marin and Tyler were showing him that.

Adam's day at the clinic seemed long, and he was struggling to get through it. His phone had been pinging with incoming messages and with phone calls received and missed, which he had been ignoring for the past few days. Finishing up with his patient reports, he neatly piled the documents to carry out to Anya's desk. She could take it from there. He then returned to his office to check his phone. He had a message from Steve Henderson, something about Jose-Luis and Geoffrey Jackson. Adam called him right away and Steve answered, but there was a great deal background noise.

"Hang on a bit, Adam, I'm just heading inside. It's loud out here."

Adam heard the sound of footsteps as Steve got to where

he needed to be, and then the din was gone.

"Thanks. There's a lot going on here right now. I'm calling to let you know that I've turned the case over to the police here in Kirkland. They'll be in touch with Buffalo to have Keith picked up and sent back here to face the music. Jose-Luis didn't hesitate to mention him when the police showed up at the hospital and walked through his door. He seems to want to lay some blame Keith's way."

Adam was thinking of Tyler and hoped he had spoken to his father right away, before the police came. It wouldn't be good if Tyler missed the opportunity to get what he needed from his dad.

Steve continued, "I might have alerted someone when I was snooping around looking for information about the two families. The cartel became afraid that Geoffrey would spill the beans. Looks like Jose-Luis had been trying to threaten Geoff to stop him from talking. It backfired when he nearly killed himself instead. Too bad he couldn't even do that right. That would have been a bit of gene pool cleansing, if you ask me. The police are leaning back to their original theory that it was Jose-Luis who killed Angie. They searched records at rental car companies and are now matching tread found at the scene to his then rental car. Anyway, I'll let you know when I have more."

"Thanks for the update, Steve."

Things had suddenly begun to happen very quickly. A grave Adam was worried that he had kicked off a chain of events that might harm either Marin or Tyler. He hoped that wasn't the case.

A few days later, Adam's phone rang and he shivered when

he looked at the call display. "Dr. Wyner? It's Tyler. Can we talk?"

"Are you okay?" There was relief mixed with concern in Adam's voice.

"The cops just came and arrested my father. We had it out, and I told him I was leaving. He didn't say anything. He didn't even ask where I was going." Tyler let out a big sigh. He seemed to have no anger left in him. "We have these notions of what our parents should be like. What all parents should be like. But then we act surprised when we discover they aren't what we thought they were. The sad thing is, when their own lives get fucked up, they take us all down with them."

"So, what will you do now?" asked Adam, sounding hopeful.

"I'm getting out of here. I'm selling my car, and I'm going to find Marin. I'm getting rid of some of my stuff; I will take the rest with me, what few things I have. But I've got money, and I'm ready to make that change. Like you said—I will accept the anxiety. You said you could help."

Adam closed his eyes and smiled when he said, "When's your birthday?"

"Twelfth of April. Why?"

39

ADAM WAS ON THE PHONE TALKING TO STEVE. THE CALL
had come early, just as Adam was heading for the door. It was
a bright, sunny day, and Adam was watching the steady drip
from the eves with the melt of the remaining snow. Spring was
in the air.

"I'm glad it worked out for everyone there, more or less,"
Steve remarked, adding, "Well, it worked out for the right
people. I'm sure both Jose-Luis and Keith are less than thrilled.
But I have to tell you that you are one tenacious SOB. I don't
know if it's confidence or stubbornness, but you got it done."

"Well, I couldn't have done it without you. I really do need
to thank you somehow." There was sincerity in Adam's voice.
He really wished he could do something for the man. "It's
really pretty exciting what you do, isn't it?"

Steve laughed his big laugh. "Oh, I don't know. Sometimes,
it's exciting. I find people, but not always. But look at you; you
help people."

It was Adam's turn to chuckle. "Yes, I help people, but like
you, not always." He then added, "Hey, if you ever plan a trip
to Toronto, let me know."

"Nah, I'm not much of a traveller. I think the last trip I took was to England as a boy, when my uncle dragged us through those shitty caves. Then I almost got killed by a car when I stepped off the curb and looked the wrong way. Don't ask me why they drive on the wrong side of the road over there. Besides, I like it here on the West Coast. There's plenty to see around here. But, if you ever come west, let me know," replied Steve with a hearty snort.

"That's a guarantee; I'll be there at some point. My parents may end up moving there, meaning I will be visiting." Adam hesitated before asking his question that he had long wanted to ask. "Can I ask you, Steve, if you believe in love at first sight? Or in the notion of a soul mate?"

Steve laughed out loud. "Where is this coming from? These kids?"

"Well, in fact, yes. It seems to have been the big question over here these past few months. I've become quite fascinated by it all, and I just thought I'd get your take as well."

"Okay, let me think." Steve's voice suddenly became more wistful. Adam figured he was enjoying this exercise, and Steve wasted no time before replying, "I wouldn't say it was love at first sight; it was probably more like lust at first sight. Like most seventeen-year-olds, the initial attraction was physical, perfect body and gorgeous to boot. I didn't think I stood a chance. But my perseverance paid off, and after a few weeks of stalking her, it wasn't illegal then, she agreed to go out with me. I think our first date was a very casual affair. On our second date, we ended up on a local park bench where we consummated our relationship with our first kiss. I can still remember that night, going home and, surprisingly, forgetting about my initial attraction and realized that there was more to this girl than my original seventeen-year-old assessment. She was smart, articulate, and caring—wow, what a combination to go with the other attributes. She was the real deal, as they say. So, it was love on first date. I wanted to protect her and care for her. I think it took her a little longer, and she wasn't as committed as I was, especially after the stalking incident. But after a few months, we became a permanent couple, and as they say, the rest is history. Thirty years later, things haven't changed all that much, still in love, still enjoy her company, although I do miss the adventure of the park bench on a cold winter night."

"That's a great story, Steve. It's a story with heart." Adam had sat quiet as he listened to Steve.

"But on a more serious note," said Steve, "I really feel for those kids. The drink can sneak up on you. I remember way back, a few of my police buddies had a party. Cards mostly. There was this one guy on the force, he really liked to drink. Well, he got really hammered that night. He wanted to drive home and we were all yelling at him to call a cab. The guy wouldn't do it. So as soon as he left, we called dispatch and had him picked up. None of us wanted it resting on our shoulders if anything had happened to him. It's serious stuff, man."

The two men hung up on a thoughtful note, wishing each other well. Adam had moved to the sofa and was now lying down with his eyes closed, thinking of Steve's story about his wife, a smile on his face. He had come to the conclusion that love was alive and well, and it would become a bigger focus with his patients. People needed to be reminded of its importance and the role it plays in communicating and healing.

Steve had informed Adam that Jose-Luis had been arrested at the hospital. He was less than agreeable about the whole thing and had some choice expletives for everyone present. Yes, he was noisy, but harmless in his present state, with both arms in casts. Keith would be transferred to Washington for questioning within a day or two, according to Steve. He would need to cooperate and provide testimony if he hoped to remain a free man. He could be a key witness and would no longer need to be afraid of retaliation. For the time being, he was safe where he was.

Steve had come to the conclusion that when Adam and Pete were poking around Keith's neighbourhood and Pete showed up on his doorstep, it must have sent panic signals.

"Keith was likely worried that Jose-Luis had found him and had sent you two snooping around. It does seem like there's more to the story, for sure."

Adam agreed. "I wondered if it was logical for the cartel to still be looking for him, particularly if he hadn't embezzled from them or betrayed them in any way. So there must be more, and I can understand Keith's fear."

Steve had supposed that Jose-Luis went after Geoffrey because he had been poking around. "Nobody likes a private dick stirring up old stuff," Steve had mused. "And there was real cause for the concern, because in the end, we did find Keith and that was exactly what the man was afraid of."

Little did the cartel know Steve originally had smaller motives when caught poking around and was quite simply trying to locate Tyler.

"Had Jose-Luis kept a low profile, he would not have been exposed. The cartel obviously believed that Geoffrey must know more than he was saying. They were convinced Angie must have told him everything before her death. They must have assumed then that Geoffrey had been talking to me, so they tried to kill him, too."

Adam found comfort knowing the police now firmly believe they could prove that he was responsible for both the death at the farmhouse and that of Angie Jackson. This hopefully would bring closure for Marin and her family.

40

ADAM AND TYLER HAD SPOKEN FREQUENTLY IN THE ensuing weeks. Tyler had not wasted any time in quitting his job and preparing for his departure. He pocketed his pay and bid goodbye to doctors and acquaintances. Dr. Denison had wished him well. According to Tyler, his mother now spent a lot of time away from the house, not wanting to be there when her son left. She chose instead to spend time at the jailhouse, visiting her husband when she wasn't working at the bistro. This in itself created a greater urgency for Tyler to leave.

Today was the day that Tyler was coming to Toronto. Adam drove to Niagara Falls to pick him up at the border crossing at Rainbow Bridge. Tyler had sold his car the previous day and had taken a cab to the border. Being early April, traffic was still quite light. Adam shielded the light from his eyes as he gazed into the crowd of oncoming pedestrians. An approaching Tyler appeared nervous as Adam waved to him.

Adam walked up to him but refrained from touching Tyler. Not even to pat him on the shoulder. Tyler's emotions were likely vulnerable, and Adam would respect his space. "You've shaved your beard. It looks good."

"Marin wouldn't like it; it's not her thing," he replied with certainty.

Reaching over to take one of Tyler's bags, Adam asked, "Is this all you have?"

Tyler smiled. "I don't own much. These are my clothes and personal things. The rest has been liquidated. My money is all in the bank and easily accessible."

"And you are sure you have a place to stay when you get there?"

Tyler nodded. "I have an old soccer friend that I can stay with. He's lining me up to see a few apartments, and I will buy a car as soon as I get there. I don't feel brave enough to drive from here; I'm still a bit of a nervous driver after what happened. And it's looking good on the job front. I've already applied online for a few positions. There's a hopeful one with Tucson Electrical Company."

Walking to where Adam had parked his car, Tyler looked at him and said, "So, no matter what happens with Marin, I'm not coming back here. We always said we'd live in Arizona, so that's where I feel I belong. Thanks for helping me get there."

Adam put Tyler's bags in the trunk and unlocked the passenger door, then turned to face him. "I don't think you need to thank me. You did this yourself. Now all you need to do is show up at Catalina State Park, and you'll find Marin."

"Aren't you coming?" Tyler looked hesitant. "Is all this for real, seriously?"

"No, I'm not going with you, and yes, it's certainly for real. My wife, Sofia, will be home in just over a week. She and I need to spend some time alone. We, too, need to start over in a sense. But I'll definitely see you in November."

"I hope she'll be there," said Tyler. "But either way, now that I know she's in Tucson, I'll know where to find her. Unless something goes wrong."

Now patting Tyler on the back, Adam stated, "Nothing will go wrong. Be positive."

That evening Adam took Tyler out for dinner, with Ben and Claire joining them. Ben appeared slightly uneasy, wondering why he needed to have a meal with this stranger, but Claire was her usual brilliant self. She had badly wanted to meet the young man. By the time they had ordered their meal, everyone had relaxed. Adam didn't ask Tyler why he chose to fly from Toronto and not Buffalo. Perhaps it was the security of having someone see him off at the airport, someone who cared and supported what he was doing. Although it felt a little awkward doing so, Adam had invited Tyler to spend the night at his house before the morning flight.

It was when they walked into the house that Tyler confessed, "You know, I came to Toronto because I thought you'd come with me."

Adam shook his head. "You will be fine; nothing will go wrong. I think you need to do this alone." And with that, the men retired for the night.

* * * *

THE FOLLOWING MORNING, ADAM WALKED to the corner to retrieve the day's mail, which he realized he had been sorely neglecting when he saw the stack. Having a cursory glance, he noticed amongst the pile a letter from El Tour de Tucson. Likely a confirmation of his registration, he thought to himself.

Returning home, he set it aside with the rest of his mail, which had also been piling up in the basket on the counter. He would have lots of time for reading through this stack once Tyler was on his way and before Sofia returned.

After a hurried coffee, they left for the airport. They arrived the same time as Claire, who had asked to be there as well. The terminal seemed unusually quiet and not the typically mad, busting place. Claire was pleased that she had insisted on coming along, and she smiled warmly at Tyler.

Adam handed Tyler a small envelope. "Here's my contact information, Tyler. It's all there. I'll see you two in November for the bike ride. We'll hike to Romero Pools together, right? Please text me when you arrive and let me know how you get settled." Tyler was nodding and smiling. He was all confidence, his face glowing.

Tyler moved into the line-up, boarding pass in hand. Just as he was disappearing around the bend, he turned and walked back over to where Adam and Claire stood. Without a word, he threw his arms around Adam's shoulders and stood there for a moment, his face pressed against Adam's body. Breaking free, he again went to his place in line, not once looking back.

Now, as they spotted Tyler walk through the customs gate, Claire put her arm through Adam's and smiled up at him. "What do you think?"

"They will figure it out. Maybe it was meant to be, maybe it wasn't. But at least now they get to decide, not someone else deciding for them. Personally, I think it will work."

Claire asked, "And how about you? Are you okay?"

"Actually, yes, I am. This has been so good for me. It's opened my eyes to things I didn't see before. This is a good thing that's happened. I think meeting that girl has changed my life."

"I think so, too," agreed Claire.

As they slowly walked to the parkade, Claire stopped walking, and after a pause, she said, without looking at him, "You know, I would have gone with you."

"Gone where?" asked Adam, gazing down at her.

Now she turned to look at him. "To Buffalo, to hand out the flyers. If Pete didn't go, I would have."

Adam laughed as he nudged her with his elbow. "Why am I not surprised? There's still a bit of detective left in you, is there? Did this bring back memories?"

"Well, Eleanor Roosevelt said we should do one thing every day that scares us. So, I guess I'm overdue," confessed Claire.

"Come on, let's go before you get me in trouble," said Adam as he swung her towards the exit doors.

Leaving the terminal, Adam could hardly believe that Tyler had just gotten on the plane to go and meet the woman of his dreams. In another week, Adam would be back here, at the airport, to collect the woman of his—Sofia was finally coming home.

He was looking forward to his wife practicing her new cooking skills on him. Claire was agog with excitement at the notion of having someone to teach her some new dishes.

Then in another four and a half months they would all be making the trip to England for the birth of Nigel and Susan's first child. He was looking forward to thanking Nigel's father I law, Joe Parrott.

But the trip he was looking forward to the most was in November, when he'd be returning to Tucson for the cycling event and the long-awaited climb to Romero Pools—hopefully with Marin and Tyler.

That evening Adam didn't feel tired. He was still reflecting on the events of the past week. Putting on the kettle, he decided to start checking his mail. He opened the first one on top of the pile: the letter from the Tucson cycling event. As he opened it, he realized it was not a confirmation document but a letter. He unfolded it and began to read, a broad smile coming over his face. It was from Marin.

"*Dear Adam. If this is the wrong Adam, I apologize and you can throw this away. If this is the correct Adam, I hope you are okay. I tried to come for dinner, but I was working, and by the time, I got there, you were gone. I tried phoning, but I didn't know your name. I know none of that matters now, but if this is you, maybe I will be lucky enough to see you at Romero Pools on the twelfth of April. If not, I will look for you in November. Your friend, Marin.*"

She had included an email address.

Adam felt moved to tears. Part of him wished he had found this letter sooner, but something inside him said it was best that he found it now, after Tyler had left.

41

THE DAY HAD ARRIVED. MARIN PULLED INTO THE PARKING lot, looking around for Adam. She was hopeful but, at the same time, was trying to curtail her optimism. Even though she had no idea if he got her letter, part of her wanted to believe he did and maybe he would be here to join her on the hike. She was beside herself with excitement, although both Penelope and Jay had warned her not to be too optimistic. It was longer than a long shot. George and Jay had offered to accompany her today, but she felt this was something she wanted to do alone. A big part of her still wanted to believe in miracles.

Coming here for today's hike was far from a triumph; it was actually quite the opposite. Today, she was saying goodbye to a big part of herself. After a few deep breaths, she opened the car door. "Let's do this," she said to herself. Two large vans were parked towards the end of the lot, a bustle of hikers swarming around, removing their gear from the hatch back. They were obscuring her view of the rest of the lot. Walking around to the trunk, she opened it to fetch her hat and water. Looking around, Marin still saw no sign of Adam. She decided to head over to the row of benches to wait for the crowd to leave. She had no intention of following on their heels, listening to their boisterous repartee all the way to the pools.

Marin had to admit that even if Adam was here somewhere, they had not coordinated a time. He could be ahead of her, or he might come behind her. She finally made the decision to head out. If she left it much longer, she would risk coming back down in the dark. She realized that wishing for Adam was a substitute for not having Tyler, and she knew it wasn't necessarily a wise thing to be wishing for. Marin walked slowly at first, but once she descended down into the wash, she felt a new energy.

Quickening her pace, she climbed the steep embankment on the other side. This was the warm-up stretch, steep enough to get anyone's heart pumping. She walked in silence, taking in the vibrant beauty around her. Ahead were the rocky slopes of the Catalina Mountains, covered with jagged outcroppings and masses of centuries-old saguaros. All around her the brush was in bloom. This was springtime in the desert, and she felt an intoxicating sense of excitement.

As Marin neared the fork in the road, she headed to the right. Her memory took her back to this spot five months ago. Just ahead of her was the area where the emergency vehicle had loaded up Adam and taken him away. Five months ago seemed like an eternity, yet it felt like yesterday. Suddenly, Adam was no longer important. She now had an alternate plan for today, one that she had been thinking about recently—a plan that was more permanent.

Marin was alone on this stretch of path. She felt happy, even though she was saying goodbye to Tyler. Peace lay ahead. Maybe she would see him again, somewhere other than earth. Marin walked slowly yet with eyes wide open at what lay ahead at the pools. She felt like a condemned man on his last walk to the gallows. But still something inside Marin spurred her on. Marin was here to say goodbye, but maybe she didn't have to. Maybe there was a way for her and Tyler to be together. It could be a good thing that she was alone today. It freed her to make this decision, to relinquish in order to begin. She looked at the sky, to where Tyler was waiting for her somewhere. She needed to stop the reeling.

With each step, it made more sense. The urging in her head had turned into a din, blocking out everything, goading her forward. This was her last journey, and she was not afraid. Nothing would matter—the job, the apartment—nothing. *Screw this,* Marin thought. Who was she kidding? She didn't want to live without Tyler. This was becoming increasingly exhausting, carrying on the charade that she was fine. All this time, her only glimmer of hope had lain with the possibility that she had overheard her father saying Tyler was alive. That hope was gone.

Suddenly, her trance was broken by a sound. Had she heard someone call her name? The sound had come from the direction of Montrose Pools. Turning in the direction of the voice, she saw an apparition. An expression of bewilderment crossed her face. Marin saw a man standing there but realized instantly that it wasn't Adam. She stared in disbelief, the tears welling up in her eyes as her legs gave out, and stumbling backwards, she sat down on the rock behind her. Was this a joke? Was she hallucinating? Was she still alive? She rubbed her eyes hard to evaporate the vision, but when she looked up, it was still there, only now it was walking towards her. Not knowing what else to do, she began to sob.

The spell was broken when the apparition spoke. She knew the voice. "I thought you'd never get here. I've been waiting for hours." Stepping even closer, the ghost smiled and said, "Actually, that's a lie. I've been waiting for years."

In three strides, Tyler was in front of her kneeling, touching her face, kissing her, a similar look of awe on his face. He stroked her hair and breathed in her scent. Then he was collapsing on the ground by her feet. He hugged her legs, and she fell forward onto him. His hair was shorter and he was thinner, but there was no illusion about who it was. She reached down to touch his head, and he was real.

"What is happening?" cried Marin, touching him all over. She was shaking, overcome with emotion.

He raised his head to look at her, his face streaked with tears. "I'm so sorry, Marin. I'm so sorry."

"It's you. It's really you. I don't understand what's going on. Where did you come from?"

"Adam sent me."

Epilogue

THE NIGHTS HAD GROWN COOL, AND THE DAYS WERE CON-siderably shorter. So much had changed in the past seven months. A nervous Marin now stood at the arrivals area, at the bottom of the escalator. She stood there, clad in her Doc Marten loafers, her khaki pants, and pinstripe blouse. Her hair was braided down her back, considerably longer than it had been at this time last year.

The flight display had indicated that the plane had landed, but as yet, the first passengers had not begun to emerge. Just as her patience was beginning to wane, she spotted a few travellers on the video monitor heading towards the escalator. She squeezed really hard, prompting a reaction from Tyler.

"Ouch, you're breaking my hand. You need to relax," he said, in a tenderly soothing voice.

Marin gazed up at him sheepishly. "Sorry, I can't believe how nervous I am. Do you think we will recognize him? I haven't seen him in a year."

Suddenly, Tyler waved his arm in the air. "There he is, Marin! I saw him on the monitor!"

She released his hand and took a few steps forward, barely refraining from running up the escalator. Then he appeared.

First his legs, and as the escalator moved, all of him came into view. There was that familiar face, wearing that familiar smile. The next second she was collapsing into Adam's arms, tears streaming down her face.

"I told myself I wouldn't cry," she said, openly sobbing at this point. She stepped back in diffidence, relaxing her hug.

Adam cupped her face in his hands. He felt like his heart could burst with happiness for her and Tyler. Turning slightly, he reached for Sofia's hand as he gently pulled her forward to make introductions.

Marin stepped towards Sofia, being careful not to crush her with enthusiasm. "I am so happy to meet you," said Marin, wiping her eyes. "There's so much to say to you both, I don't even know where to start."

"We will have lots of time for that," Sofia responded with a smile.

Adam gazed at his wife. Such an intensely profound scene had just unfolded, and the agreeable surprise was evident on Sofia's face.

Tyler stepped forward to greet both Sofia and Adam, whose hand he shook warmly. Adam noticed the change in Tyler's grip. It was a good, strong, confident handshake.

"It's a real pleasure to meet you, Sofia," said Tyler softly. "You have an amazing husband." Tyler stood proudly beside Marin, his arm around her, the two of them seeming as one. Their connectedness was evident.

"You both look really well," commented Adam. "I mean, really, really well!" The two faces that beamed back at him, in this light, almost had an aura emanating around them, although Adam was sure he was imagining it.

Luggage was collected, and within minutes, they were outside in the warm Arizona air. Adam lifted his face to the sky and, with eyes closed, inhaled his surroundings. It felt so good to be back in the blazing heat of the desert. Bring on the dryness and the dust and the prickly pear, not to mention the blowtorch temperatures. It felt fantastic to be here once again, and he was happy to sharing it with Sofia.

Tyler had selected a hotel nearer to their home in Oro Valley that promised magnificent views of the mountains and would be close to the starting point of the El Tour de Tucson ride. Adam turned to Marin and said, "So, we are ready to do this bike ride tomorrow. Short route only, right? Sofia is looking forward to it." Sofia grinned at Marin and nodded excitedly.

Tyler moved to the back of the car and helped Adam put the luggage in the trunk. "And then we are hiking to Romero Pools the day after that; I hope nobody has forgotten. By the way, Marin has invited two friends to join us—Jay and George. I don't know if she told you they were coming, but she wanted them to be with us. She wants them to meet you, Adam. She mentioned something about a milagro?"

Acknowledgements

MY EXPLORATION INTO LOVE AND RELATIONSHIPS WAS EYE opening and, at times, enviable. I have spoken to many couples that have been together for most of their lives, many since the age of eighteen or nineteen. Their love stories are heartwarming. I won't list you by name, but you know who you are. A special thank-you to Robert—I loved your story and seeing you both together now, forty-seven years later, is a testament to the endurance of that story.

To Frank Giampa, no words are needed. Our friendship is eternal and your support has been immeasurable.

To my readers, thank you so much for making my dream of writing come true.

Book Club Questions

1. Do you believe in the notion of a soul mate, or love at first sight?

2. What did you like best about the book?

3. What did you like least?

4. Which characters in the book did you like best?

5. Did you like the idea of having two main characters' points of view?

6. If you were making a movie of this book, whom would you cast?

7. Share a favorite quote from the book. Why did this quote stand out?

8. What other books by this author have you read? How did they compare to this book?

9. Would you read another book by this author? Why or why not?

10. What feelings did this book evoke for you?

11. What songs does this book make you think of? Create a book group playlist together!

12. If you got the chance to ask the author of this book one question, what would it be?

13. Which character in the book would you most like to meet?

14. Which places in the book would you most like to visit?

15. What do you think of the book's title? How does it relate to the book's contents? What other title might you choose?

16. What do you think the author's purpose was in writing this book? What ideas was he or she trying to get across?

17. How original and unique was this book?

18. How well did the author build the world in the book?

About the Author

ALYSSA HALL WAS BORN AND RAISED in Newmarket, Ontario, but she now lives in Langley, British Columbia, with her husband, David. Alyssa writes from the heart and about places and themes she knows well. Her third novel, *Romero Pools*, takes the reader on a journey from the Toronto area to Tucson and Oro Valley, where Alyssa and David have been snowbirds for the past fourteen years. She has spent much of her time exploring the areas.

Also the author of *Wanting Aidan* (FriesenPress, April 2021) and *Trusting Claire* (FriesenPress, December 2020), Alyssa expertly weaves characters from these two books into her third. Although each book is individual and unique and can be read in any order, having knowledge of the characters may enhance the story for the reader. Find out more about Alyssa and her books at her website: www.alyhallwriter.com.

CPSIA information can be obtained
at www.ICGtesting.com
Printed in the USA
LVHW041659120322
713134LV00011B/1169

9 781039 131